Blaze®

Dear Reader,

Although I have written more than fifty books over the past decade, I have never stopped feeling a special fondness for the stories about a very special family, the Santoris of Chicago. I wrote the first Santori story way back in 2001. The hero's name was Joe, he was the second oldest in a family of six kids, and he was a blue collar construction worker who fell in love with a sweet-natured teacher. I loved Joe from day one and still consider him one of my best heroes.

I never intended to write more stories about the family, until a couple of years later, when readers began asking me what had happened to all those siblings. So I did a cute little story about Lucas, the third son. I really enjoyed writing that story, and so I came up with stories for all the siblings. The last one came out in 2008. Since then, I've occasionally referred to the clan or had a family member pop up in another, unrelated book, but I'd never really focused on them again until last year. Readers seemed to want more of this big Italian family, and I decided to explore the idea of another branch on the Santori family tree. Deciding on a family with three sons, I had a fantastic time writing about Leonardo (Leo, *Lying in Your Arms*), Rafael (Rafe, *A Soldier's Christmas*) and Michaelangelo (Mike, *Double Take*). I loved these big, strong, sexy guys and the women who tamed them.

You might have noticed that the stories do not take place in Chicago. I intended to revisit the family, but wanted these books to have a very different feel from the original six. That's why these three Santori boys find love outside of Chicago, and why you don't see a lot of the "old" characters (though, the appearance of the twins, Nick and Mark, in this book, is one of my favorite scenes!)

I hope you enjoy getting to visit with this big, crazy family again. Who knows? Maybe in a few years we'll see what the next generation of Santori men is up to!

Happy reading!

Leslie

Leslie Kelly

—

Double Take

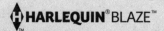

Recycling programs
for this product may
not exist in your area.

ISBN-13: 978-0-373-79799-8

DOUBLE TAKE

Printed in U.S.A.

HARLEQUIN®
www.Harlequin.com

ABOUT THE AUTHOR

New York Times bestselling author Leslie Kelly has written dozens of books and novellas for the Harlequin Blaze, Temptation and HQN lines. Known for her sparkling dialogue, fun characters and steamy sensuality, she has been honored with numerous awards, including a National Readers' Choice Award, a Colorado Award of Excellence, a Golden Quill and an *RT Book Reviews* Career Achievement Award in Series Romance. Leslie has also been nominated four times for the highest award in romance fiction, the RWA RITA® Award. Leslie lives in Maryland with her own romantic hero, Bruce, and their daughters.

Visit her online at www.lesliekelly.com or at her blog, www.plotmonkeys.com.

Books by Leslie Kelly

HARLEQUIN BLAZE

To get the inside scoop on Harlequin Blaze and its talented writers, be sure to check out www.blazeauthors.com.

To my dear old high school friends

Lori, Kim, Linda, Rick, Ed, Chris...and so many others.

I'm so thankful for the memories we made so long ago and the new ones we're creating today.

Prologue

"WE'RE ASKING YOU to take an extended leave of absence."

Lindsey Smith flinched, even though she had expected the words. She had, in fact, steeled herself for them before she'd taken a seat across from her boss, eminent psychotherapist Walter Ross, of the Ross, Riley and Wilhelm Wellness Center. She had to wonder if the other two partners had drawn the long straws, leaving Ross to take care of "their little problem."

"It's not that serious," she argued, but in her head she was screaming, *This is so serious, your reputation is crap!* "It will die down."

"So you've been saying, Dr. Smith. But that was before you became the subject of a *Jeopardy!* question."

Well, in her opinion, being on *Jeopardy!* had been kind of awesome, though she wasn't going to tell her employer that. "But…"

"And today I was informed you're the subject of a me-me."

"A what-what?"

Ross pushed a sheet of paper toward her across his desk, using only the tips of his fingers, as if the paper offended him.

She scanned the sheet. Huh. *She* was the one who should

be offended. Her picture appeared on the page, over and over, each time with a witty—but so not funny—quip. She read, "Had an orgasm while blinking," and, "Comes when going," before snapping, "It's pronounced *meem*."

"However you say the word, it reflects badly on us all."

"You read my dissertation before you hired me."

He nodded. "I know. It was fine research. Your work with patients with sexual disorders has been outstanding."

But not outstanding enough for them to defend her when she caught some unpleasant attention. Oh, sure, at first her bosses had enjoyed the publicity when excerpts of her dissertation on women's ability to climax merely via mental stimulation had hit the media. But when the *Today* show got on it, followed by the tabloids, they'd tensed up.

Things got worse when the internet fell on her head. "Thinkgasm," the word she'd used to describe mind-initiated climax, had trended on Twitter and she'd become a laughingstock.

Now, because of a game-show question and a stupid meme, they were abandoning her to deal with it on her own. During her "leave of absence," they'd undoubtedly be watching like Big Brother to see if she could stay "clean" enough to renew their association with her sometime in the future. All because she took seriously what so many found funny: female orgasms.

So much for being a champion for women taking control of their lives, their bodies and their sexuality. Her own life was spinning out of control, courtesy of the man in front of her and other men just like him. It infuriated her.

If there was one thing Lindsey hated, it was being made to feel powerless to shape her own destiny. *Been there, done that.* She'd fought hard to make sure nobody had that kind of dominance over her. Only to come to this.

Ross pasted on his calm, therapist smile. "It'll be all

right, Dr. Smith. Just try to stay out of the limelight, and in a couple of months we'll revisit things. Why don't you go away for a while? Leave Chicago. Go somewhere quiet, remote, where your name isn't going to grab such immediate attention."

"Where might that be?" she asked, not hiding her sarcasm. "The dark side of the moon?"

It seemed everybody and his uncle had heard her name, and cracked-up over the *silly* idea that a woman's imaginings could be enough to give her physical, sexual pleasure. Could there be a place left in the country where she wasn't a joke, where she could live in anonymity and protect her privacy from prying eyes and gossipy rumor mills?

She honestly didn't know. But considering she was temporarily unemployed, heartsick and living under a spotlight, it was time to find out.

1

Three Weeks Later

THE REDHEAD in the green raincoat would be very pretty if she weren't about to lose her lunch over the side of the ferry. Hell, not just pretty, beautiful, with those wide-set eyes, the high cheekbones, the curvaceous figure and that stunning head of long, flowing red hair.

Right now, though, her face was about the same shade as her coat. Her mouth was a tight little knot of agony. And her hands clenched the railing as if she couldn't decide whether to throw up or just jump overboard and put herself out of her misery.

Eyeing her from a few feet down the railing, to which he was also clinging with only slightly less desperation, Mike Santori offered her a look of commiseration and sympathy.

"First time heading to the island?" he asked, raising his voice to be heard over the rumble of the engine, the whipping of the wind and the spray of the water flying off the surface of Lake Michigan.

She managed a tiny nod, groaning aloud as if even that slight movement was too much for her spinning head.

"Maybe you should go inside."

"No, I need the fresh air!"

He understood that. He, too, had to remain outside every time he made the crossing between the island and the mainland. He kept hearing that the trek to and from his new home on Wild Boar Island would get easier, that he'd even grow to like it. But so far the only improvement he'd managed was that he no longer had to curl up in the fetal position on one of the outside benches and pray. The day he actually grew to enjoy the journey was the day he started to enjoy getting his prostate checked by anybody other than an adventurous girlfriend.

"It's going to start raining in a minute," he warned her, wondering if she, like him, would be glad for the rain. At least when you were shaking from being cold and drenched, you could forget your head was spinning as if somebody had attached a string to it and was using it as a yo-yo.

"Maybe I'll get lucky and the storm will wash me overboard so I can drown."

"Please don't, then I'd have to jump in and save you, and I'll ruin my new boots."

She managed a weak smile. But it quickly faded when the ferry dipped, rolling on a swell that made the rickety old boat sound as though it was going to split apart at the seams and plunge to Davy Jones's locker. The redhead gripped even tighter, and a low groan escaped her lips. "Make it stop."

"We're almost there," he said, edging closer, feeling protective of her, this pretty stranger, the way he might have of a kid left outside in the cold.

"What is wrong with good old-fashioned bridges?"

"It's twelve miles to the island."

"Haven't they heard of the Donghai?"

"What's that?"

"It's a bridge that's twenty miles long."

"Across Lake Michigan?"

She rolled her eyes. He bit back a smile, glad he was distracting her.

Another dip. Another groan. "There's an even longer one going over Lake Pontchartrain," she said, forcing the words out from between clenched teeth.

That one he had heard of. "I hear they get a few more tourists to New Orleans than they do to Wild Boar Island. I don't think tolls would pay for a bridge here."

That was an understatement.

Wild Boar Island, Michigan, his new home as of a few months ago, might claim it was one of the most popular tourist destinations in the state during the summer months. Hell, it might even be true. But somehow, having a population that swelled from about eighteen-hundred nine months out of the year up to ten-thousand in June, July and August, didn't quite equal the Big Easy during Mardi Gras.

A strong gust of wind blew down from the thunderous storm clouds blanketing the sky—clouds which hadn't yet released a torrent of rain, but had done a fine job whipping the massive lake into a trembling ocean. The old ferry rocked and rolled like a theme-park ride, and his stomach rocked and rolled along with it.

"Oh, God, why did I ever agree to move to a place you can only get to by ferry?" she groaned, leaning over the railing.

She leaned a bit too far, gasping and heaving, and he had a sudden vision of her tipping head-first into the choppy green wake. He didn't know her from Adam, but he sure wasn't about to watch her take a nose-dive into the deep. So he stepped close behind her, shielding her body with his own and wrapping an arm around her waist to hold her steady, braced on the deck. He dropped a free hand onto one of hers and squeezed, hoping she got the message that he was just trying to help and wasn't some pervert going for an easy grope.

Not that the woman wasn't eminently touchable.

He could feel shudders wracking her tall, slim form, even through her heavy raincoat. But she made no effort to pull away, and instead gripped his hand.

"We're going to capsize," she groaned.

"No, we aren't."

"Yes, we are. We're going to flip over and sink."

"Well, at least then we won't feel sick anymore."

She glanced at him over her shoulder, long strands of wind-blown red hair whipping across her face. "You, too?"

"Why do you think I'm out here?"

"I figured it was so you could rescue me."

"Yeah, let's go with that," he said as the ferry bounced again and he let out a small groan of his own.

She laughed suddenly, a light, musical peal of merriment that was at odds with the wild, wind-whipped day. Her whole face lit up when she laughed, and he noted the sparkle in her eyes, which were a dazzling shade of emerald.

"Are you laughing at me?" he asked, torn between indignation and relief that she no longer looked like she was about to jump overboard.

"Nope." She lifted a slender hand and pointed. "I'm laughing with sheer relief because I see land ahead!"

"Hate to break it to you, but that's Little Boar, not Wild Boar."

"Close enough. I'm getting off."

"The ferry doesn't stop there—it's uninhabited."

"I'll take my chances with the little boars, just tell the captain to pull over."

"There's nowhere to dock."

"So I'll jump overboard and swim for it."

"Have you forgotten my new boots?"

"You'd really leap in after me?"

"It's in my job description."

"Are you a lifeguard?"

Lately he'd been a jack-of-all-trades—from cat-rescuer, to crossing guard, to 911 operator—as well as Chief of Police, his official title. And he didn't imagine lifeguarding would be out of the question this summer when Wild Boar filled up with tourists anxious to test the sometimes rough waters of this very great lake.

"Let's just say I'm your self-appointed lifeguard right now. If you jump, I jump."

She took a few deep breaths, letting his words calm her, as he'd wanted them to. Finally, she nodded and began to straighten. The chop had died down, at least momentarily, and the planking seemed steadier beneath his feet. At least, it did as long as he didn't think about how easily his arm encircled her slim waist and how her long legs felt when practically entwined with his. And if he dwelled on the way her curvy ass was brushing against his groin, he was a total goner. The dizziness would have nothing to do with the waves and everything to do with a hot rush of lust that threatened to drown him. As a matter of fact, the tide was lifting things up already.

Mike immediately let her go and stepped away, willing himself back into she's-a-stranger mode and out of the damn-she's-hot one.

"Do you think the water's calming down now?" she asked, pushing her tangled hair away from her face with a shaking hand.

"Seems like it."

"God, I hate being sick like that."

"Ditto."

She eyed him. "It's not just the nausea, it's the complete lack of control over it. I know when I step off this boat, it'll go away—mostly. And it infuriates me that I can't make it go away right now."

He grinned. "If you can come up with a method to think away nausea, you'll be rich."

She nibbled her lip and looked down, crossing her arms and shivering lightly. Still not looking at him, she murmured, "Maybe we'll have smooth sailing the rest of the way?"

"Absolutely."

Nope. This was more like the eye of the hurricane. Experience told him they were merely enjoying a moment of respite before they hit the big swells that encircled Wild Boar. The island currents made travel in the winter and early spring—which was now—dangerous and nausea-inducing. But he didn't tell her that.

"I can't believe we're the only ones out here on deck. How could anybody not be seasick after that?"

He gestured toward the car-park section of the ferry, empty but for a shiny yellow Prius, which he assumed was hers. *Good luck finding a charging station on Wild Boar.* He'd left his own SUV at the docks, as his errand to the mainland to deliver some paperwork to the nearest county sheriff's station had been a quick one. It had been easier to just have one of the county guys pick him up and drop him back off than deal with the hassle of taking his vehicle with him.

"We're the only customers on board. The rest are crew and they're used to it. This time of year I doubt they get more than one or two people a trip."

"What? I thought we were heading to the most happening island this side of Maui."

"Who told you that?" he asked with a grin. "Somebody who desperately needs you to take over their job for a while?"

She lifted a brow, studying him, as if hearing the certainty in his voice. That could be because he *was* now certain of who this beautiful, red-haired stranger was, and why she was heading to a remote, sparsely-populated island on this wickedly unpleasant day. "Is Monday your first day at the school?"

Her eyes popped; she appeared shocked he'd hit the nail on its proverbial head.

"You *are* the new teacher, aren't you?" he asked, even though he knew he was right. The island had been agog all week about some mainlander coming to teach the science classes at the island's one and only school, which catered to all five-hundred or so students, from kindergarten through twelfth grade.

"Sub," she clarified. "I'm only substituting for the rest of the semester for my old friend who's the regular teacher."

Right. He hadn't met her yet, but of course he'd heard all about Mrs. Parker, the science teacher. The woman's baby had been born ten weeks premature and was still in an ICU unit on the mainland. That's why there'd been a sudden need for a substitute, and those weren't easy to come by on Wild Boar. Especially not teachers qualified to teach every science class in the school, from first grade why-do-caterpillars-turn-into-butterflies clear through advanced chemistry. Why this one wasn't already tied up in a classroom three-quarters of the way through the current school year, he couldn't say, but he had to admit he was interested in learning more about her.

"How did you know who I was?"

"There's been lots of concern for your friend and her new baby. Concern equals talk on Wild Boar."

"Callie's baby is doing well," the woman said with a

gentle smile that softened her pale, pinched expression. "Little Will's got a lot of growing to do, and his lungs aren't fully developed, but the doctors think he's out of the woods."

"I'm glad to hear it."

She nodded. "Me, too. He's deeply loved and was very much wanted." She glanced away. "Unlike a lot of children."

He noted the change of tone and wondered at it. But she didn't give him a chance to wonder long.

"Still, how did you know *I* was the new teacher?"

"It's pretty rare for newcomers to move out to the island, except for the summer tourist folks, and it's too early for them. Plus, everybody's talking about the cottage behind the old Wymer place being rented out for the next couple of months."

He didn't have the heart to tell her that the cottage was ancient, rickety, drafty and probably full of spiders. Hopefully Mrs. Wymer had hired somebody to clean it up, since the fragile-looking elderly woman certainly couldn't do it herself.

The stranger's pale face became a shade closer to chalky. "Good grief, is the whole island a gossip mill?"

"Yeah, and that thing's been grinding like crazy with all the new arrivals—that'd be you and me."

She glanced down, one of her slim hands fisting as she pressed it into her stomach, as if she felt nauseous. Well, he supposed that was understandable.

"You're a newcomer, too?" she finally asked, after she'd straightened her back and lifted her chin.

"Yes, ma'am." He extended a hand. "I'm Mike."

"Lindsey." She took his hand and shook. Hers was a little clammy and very cold, since she'd been gripping the damp metal railing.

He reached into the pockets of his bulky windbreaker and pulled out his utility gloves, shoving them toward her. "Here. Your fingers are icicles."

She stared down at his offering. "Don't you need them?"

"I want my hands bare so I can clutch that railing," he said with a wry grin.

"If I wear your gloves, how am *I* going to hold on?"

"How about I hold on for us both?"

"Pretty confident, are you?"

"I think I can manage to keep us from being swept overboard."

She cast a quick eye over his shoulders, chest and arms. Color finally rose into those pale cheeks, as if she'd at last looked at him and seen the man, not the savior-from-death-by-drowning-or-seasickness. Her throat quivered as she swallowed, her gaze dropping lower, assessing him all the way down to his feet.

"I suppose you can," she admitted, her voice thick and low.

He almost made a flirtatious comment in response, but suddenly the ferry lurched again, making him glad for his strong grip on the railing. But the woman—Lindsey— wobbled on her feet and, for a second, he thought she'd fall. Not even thinking about it, he stepped into her path and grabbed her before she could stumble.

Their legs tangled, hips bumped and chests collided. He had a chance to suck in a shocked—and pleased—breath, when her fine red hair whipped across his face, bringing with it a flowery fragrance that cut through the briny air and went right to his head. Just like this woman was doing.

"Whoa," she murmured, either because of the stumbling or the fact that so much of her was now touching so much of him.

"I've got you," he said, placing a firm hand on her

shoulder. He turned his back to the wind, staying close, but giving her some distance and disengaging the more vulnerable parts of their bodies. As nice as she had felt pressed against him, he didn't want her to know that his lower half was ignoring his brain's order to be a polite protector and was instead going straight for horny man. Their new position removed the danger of sensual overload, but also kept her blocked from the worst of the wind. "I won't let you fall overboard. Now glove up."

Not taking no for an answer, he lifted one of her small, cold hands and shoved a glove on it. He forced himself to focus only on the fact that her lips now had a bluish tint, not that they were pretty damned kissable. And that her expression was pure misery, not that her face was shaped like a perfect heart, with high cheekbones and a pointy, stubborn little chin.

Once her hands were adequately protected, she stepped the tiniest bit closer, as if welcoming the shelter of his body. Mike heaved in a deep breath of cold lake air, but found it tasted of spicy-fragranced woman.

Nice. Very nice.

"So, how long have you lived on Wild Boar?" she asked.

"A few months."

"And how's island life?"

He considered it, mentally comparing the insanely quiet nights he'd spent on Wild Boar to the lifetime of noise, energy, grime and vibrancy in Chicago.

"It's…different."

"Obviously you're getting to know people if they're already gossiping to you about the new substitute teacher."

"Maybe. It could also be because we're two new unmarried people and they're trying to set us up."

Her mouth fell open. "They're *what?*"

"Apparently your friend—the one you're substituting for—has let it be known that you are single and available."

"Remind me to smack her, would you?"

"You bet."

She licked her lips. "So you're single, too?"

He noticed she didn't add *and available,* maybe because she didn't want to sound interested, though he could tell she was. Oh, she might not be looking at him, instead taking every chance she had to study her gloved hands, but he recognized desire when he saw it. During those few moments when she'd landed hard against him, heat had flared between them, instinctive and powerful.

"I'm *very* single," he admitted, not sure why he'd emphasized it. After all, he should be backing away from flirtation or even the tiniest hint of romantic interest. He had no business indulging in either right now.

"And everybody is aware you're single?"

"Yep. Just like they know your relationship status. Or lack thereof."

"I can't believe Callie told everyone that."

"Well, to be fair, I suspect she told one person and the other eighteen-hundred residents found out by osmosis."

Because that's how news traveled in a small town. When he'd come to Wild Boar for his job interview, he certainly hadn't gone around saying he was unattached. By the time he'd moved there to start the job, however, it had been common knowledge to every person he met.

Of all the things he disliked about his new life, the utter lack of privacy ranked number one. In fact, he hated feeling as if he lived under a microscope, and wasn't about to give the gossipers any more ammunition if he could possibly help it. He needed to keep his life quiet, sedate and boring. Meaning no leaping off ferries to save gorgeous, impetuous redheads. So she'd better not jump.

"You're an expert on osmosis, huh? Why aren't *you* the substitute science teacher?"

He chuckled. "I have a rough idea of what the word means, but ask me to explain the difference between oxygen and iron and I'm in deep trouble."

"One you breathe and one you make stuff out of."

Another chuckle. "My point is, you're not getting off so easily."

She nodded slowly, and he couldn't tell if she was relieved by that, or bothered by it.

"And if it's any consolation, you're not alone in the gossip pool. I'm treading water right there with you."

She rolled her eyes and gestured toward the waves. "Could we please use another analogy?"

Damn, he enjoyed her wit. "Okay, let's say I'm just as big a grape dangling from that huge, gossipy vine. Every day since I arrived, I've had cakes, cookies and casseroles brought to my doorstep by the population of single women on the island, ranging in age from eighteen to eighty."

"Has it worked?"

"I haven't taken the bait yet."

Her cheeks puffed out as she feigned sickness. "No fish references, either, please."

"Fish aren't the only ones who eat bait."

"But single men often do. Have you? Eaten the food, I mean? There could be secret love potions hidden inside."

"That's possible. There's one widow, Mrs. Cranston— gotta be seventy if she's a day—who makes the best lemon meringue pie I've ever tasted. I might propose to her even without the love potion."

They laughed together, both of them distracted, for a little while, anyway, from the misery of their journey.

"I wonder what they'll bring me. I don't suppose I'll be inundated with cakes and pies from the single men."

"Maybe you'll get cans of baked beans. Or motor oil."

"Small-town hell. Check."

"I wouldn't go so far as to call it hell. More like a really claustrophobic closet in the middle of an island."

"With eighteen-hundred people in it."

"Exactly." And didn't that sound appealing?

You decided to come here. You wanted a total do-over. Yeah. Right. He had.

He'd been the one who wanted a change, the one so anxious to get out of Chicago—to escape from the darkness, the blood, the anger and the nonstop violence. It had been nobody's choice but his own to quit his job of eight years with the Chicago P.D., to leave his upwardly mobile career as a detective.

He'd seen the ad for a Chief of Police of Tiny Island, Nowhere, and jumped on it, not really sure what he wanted or where he was going, just sure that after near misses with at least three bullets and a direct hit with a switchblade, he had to get away for his own sanity. And for his parents', who'd pleaded with him to find another—safer—career.

Of course, they hadn't intended for it to be so far away from them. He wasn't sure if they'd call Wild Boar an improvement, considering he was the first Santori of his generation to actually move out of Illinois. But considering his parents had their first grandbaby to look forward to, courtesy of his brother Leo and his new wife, he supposed he wasn't on their minds 24/7.

Besides, he couldn't say if this would be a long-term change or not. He was well into his probationary period, having agreed to stay on the job for a minimum of six months. At the end of that time, either he, or the island's authorities, could make a change, no harm, no foul. No matter how often he'd wondered if he'd made the biggest mistake of his life, he would keep his word on that. He'd see how he felt at the end of the six months, and then make some decisions for his future.

Mike wanted it to work out. He couldn't stand the thought of going back to the Chicago P.D. An optimist like him could only stick it out for so long in a job where he couldn't make a difference before it became agony to go to work every day. Maybe on Wild Boar he wasn't saving lives, but he made a difference in little ways. In Chicago, the only life he'd managed to save was his own, and that had been a struggle every Goddamn day of the week.

His spirit had been crushed by it. Day after day he'd seen the same brutal crimes, the same utter disregard for other people's lives and property, the same hopelessness and despair. It had become an agony to go to work every day.

Wild Boar was the complete opposite. Peaceful, tranquil, a place where neighbors helped neighbors and everybody knew every other person on the island.

True, he didn't love it yet, or even like it that much. He was too much of a Chicagoan for that. He was hopeful, though, that one day he'd wake up and realize he'd become a true islander and want to stick around for a few years. Or twenty.

Sometimes he even pictured himself asking one of those nice, pie-making women out, giving this life a real shot. Maybe he'd get married, do the whole family thing with the picket fence and pot-roast dinners on Sunday. The matchmakers on Wild Boar certainly seemed to want that future for him. And, unlike his last girlfriend, a nice, small-town woman from Wild Boar Island would probably be happy with that kind of life. He couldn't deny, part of him found that idea very appealing, too.

Of course, another part wanted to jump off this ferry right now and swim back to the mainland.

No. You're sticking this out.

He just had to keep his head down, do his job, and focus on figuring out what he *really* wanted before someone else decided for him. He definitely didn't need complications—like romantic entanglements—to interfere with the decision-making process.

"So the matchmakers are a powerful force, I take it?"

"Oh, yes."

"Listen, Mike, I'm only going to be on the island for a short time and I'm not looking for…"

He assumed she was about to let him down easy and he put a hand up, palm out, heading her off at the rejection. Not that he'd tried to, er, lift himself up. "Say no more. I said the gossipers are pairing us up, not that I wanted them to. You are perfectly safe from me."

Her spine might have stiffened the tiniest bit. Hard to tell beneath her coat, and he realized he might have insulted her. Damn, he was so not used to this, though he should be. When it came to matchmaking, the entire population of Wild Boar Island had nothing on the Santori family. Whenever he was between relationships, his mother, aunts and cousins were always pushing females in his direction—blond, brunette, divorcées, partying singles—if she had a pulse but not a ring, they sent her his way.

But he couldn't recall them ever introducing him to one with hair that vivid shade of red or eyes that brilliant, glittering green, or one with such luscious—if blue-tinged—lips.

He tried to explain himself. "Look, I didn't mean anything. It's just, you're…"

"It's okay," she said with a shrug and an understanding nod. "You're gay, no problem."

His mouth unhinged. "I'm *what?*"

She nibbled on her bottom lip. "Uh, you're not gay?"

"Definitely not," he said, torn between amusement and horror. "And if you tell me I give off a gay vibe, I might go ahead and leap, new boots be damned."

Then he frowned. Worrying about his boots... That was a pretty metrosexual thing to do, wasn't it? Shit. How was a guy to know?

"You don't give off a vibe," she insisted. "I just made an assumption based on what you said."

"You think just because a guy's not interested in you, he likes dudes?" He was baiting her; she didn't come across as the vain type, but then one never knew.

"That did sound conceited, didn't it?" she asked, visibly embarrassed. "I'm really sorry. I'm not thinking straight. It's just that you said I was 'safe' from you, that you were single, completely available and that every unattached woman in town has come on to you. I just figured..."

"You figured wrong. I'm simply not in the market. New job, new town, new home. No privacy on this postage stamp of an island. There's just too much on my plate right now and I can't afford any distractions while I try to negotiate myself through this new life I've chosen for myself."

Although, if he did have an empty plate, he could picture this woman sitting right in the middle of it, all sweet and succulent, just waiting to be devoured.

Forget it. Not happening. He was burned out on romance these days. Well, he'd had it burned *out* of him, and by a woman he'd believed he could get serious with. She'd chosen her big-league banking job over him even *before* he'd decided to leave Chicago. She had made it pretty clear that her ritzy cocktail parties and corporate events weren't the place for a guy who carried a gun and had a fresh razor-blade scar across his neck. Nice news for somebody lying in a hospital bed.

He was also not in the market for a new girlfriend because he lived under a microscope. "Hate to break it to you, Red, but if you and I so much as went out on an ice-cream date, the word would be all over the Wild Boar grapevine before I got in one good lick of my Rocky Road."

Or your Cookies 'n Cream.

He didn't add that, wishing the more flirtatious voice in his head would back off and leave the driving to his more reasonable side.

"I understand. And ditto. Definitely not in the market for any complications."

"Good. Then there's no problem."

They understood each other. Which was fine. Perfect. They'd be neighborly, friendly. Nothing else.

Something deep inside him tried to throw up a penalty flag at that prospect, but he shoved it away and focused on doing what was smart, not what was desirable.

They were close to the island now, and, as he'd expected, the rickety old ferry suddenly got caught in the surging current that swirled around it. The craft lunged up, and then slammed back down. Despite the steadying presence of his hand on her shoulder, Lindsey couldn't keep her feet totally grounded. She stumbled forward, falling against him with a startled cry.

Thank heaven he was there, or she might actually have tumbled over the railing into the drink. Instead, Mike caught her in his arms, holding her close, not content with a hand on her shoulder while the chop was this rough.

They both gasped, startled by the close call, the crazy weather, the sway of the boat. And, for Mike, by her nearness.

This wasn't just the lining-up of certain body parts, he was actually holding her in his arms. One was wrapped around her waist, a hand cupping her hip, the other encircling her shoulders. Every inch of her touched every inch of him. Each cell in his body reacted, parts of him awakening that he'd thought would remain in hibernation at least until he'd made a place for himself on Wild Boar Island.

Uh-uh. Despite the cold air and the colder water, the rocking of the boat and the rolling of his stomach, he looked down into those big green eyes, felt the press of that soft, female form, and realized something.

This red-haired beauty was indeed going to be a complication. A very serious complication.

2

FOR THE PAST few years, ever since her best friend, Callie, had gotten married and moved to an island in the Great Lakes, Lindsey had promised to visit. More than once, she'd made plans to come for a week between semesters, or even a long weekend.

But something had always come up—schoolwork, research, her job. Once, there'd been a fellowship opportunity, another time she'd been offered a prestigious study abroad. For the past two summers, Lindsey had been asked to work seventy hours a week, rather than her usual fifty, to cover for one of the partners' vacations. As much as she loved Callie, and wanted to get to know her husband, Billy, she'd just never been able to make it work, because of *work*.

Now, though, she was going, and nothing would stop her. Her friend needed her, and Lindsey wasn't going to let Callie down. She hadn't had many friends during her childhood; hell, she didn't really have many now. Callie had always been the best of them, and still was.

The two of them had gravitated to each other in kindergarten, both poor kids who wore secondhand clothes and had firsthand chips on their shoulders. They'd dared anyone to look down on them. Of course, Callie's parents had been loving and hardworking, and had done the best they could for their daughter.

Lindsey's? Well, not so much. Neglectful would probably be the nicest way to refer to their parenting style. Emotionally abusive wouldn't be too far off the mark.

She'd never seen much in the way of love in her own house, and hadn't been entirely sure she recognized it when she later spotted it in Callie's. Still, the two of them had been inseparable through high school graduation. After that, Callie had decided to stay close to home. Lindsey had been determined to go *anywhere* else, as long as it was someplace that didn't include an absolute dearth of trust, intimacy and tenderness. Like home.

She'd clawed her way into the Ivy League with sheer determination and excellent grades, being the poster child for poor-kid-makes-good. She'd worked hard, methodically controlling every aspect of her life, allowing nothing to distract her from her goals. Her parents hadn't been around to see her succeed—her father had taken off more than a decade ago, and her mother had died when Lindsey was twenty.

Callie, though, had been there every step of the way, even if they only connected by phone. The disparate paths their lives had taken couldn't ever change the genuine connection they had. They were sisters in every way except biologically.

Now, with a preemie baby in the hospital fighting to survive, the last thing Callie needed to worry about was whether she had a job to go back to in the fall. And Callie had been right to worry. Given its size, the Wild Boar Community School couldn't go without a science teacher for an entire quarter.

Her friend was supposed to have given birth at the end of the school year, and then have the summer off for maternity leave. Now, though, with almost another full grading term to go, the school board had been panicked. Nobody on the island was qualified to teach the wide variety of science classes, and nobody off it would be willing to move for just a short-term position. So they'd informed her friend that if she had to take more time off work than her allotted leave, they might have to hire a full-time replacement and try to find another spot for Callie the next school year.

As a result, Callie had spent too many hours worrying about her job, when she should be worried only about her health and her son. Lindsey was not about to let her expend any more energy on career woes. If Lindsey hadn't been forced into her not-so-voluntary sabbatical, she might not have been able to work it out. As it was, though, she had the time and the desire to help.

Since it was a substitute position and they were under pressure to hire someone quickly, there hadn't been too many hoops for Lindsey to jump through. The school officials had confirmed she had a Bachelor's Degree from Johns Hopkins, with a double major in Chemistry and Biology, and leaped on her offer to be a short-term sub. They didn't even know about her PhD.

Only after she'd agreed to do it had she realized Wild Boar Island might also be the answer to her own prayer. Callie's remote slice of heaven, which she'd always gushed about in her emails and phone calls, had internet access and TV, but, as far as her friend knew, they weren't talking about Dr. Lindsey Smith and her Thinkgasms. The administrators hadn't said a word about it during her phone interview, or questioned why she was not currently employed. She suspected they subscribed to the don't-look-a-gift-horse-in-the-mouth adage. It was entirely possible she'd actually found a place in the country where she wasn't being laughed at or whispered about.

"Oh, please let that be true," she mumbled, tired beyond belief of being fodder for the scandal-happy, soft-story media.

Even if it wasn't, she'd still have come to the island. Callie needed her. Not many people had ever needed her, and Lindsey wasn't about to turn away someone she loved who so desperately did.

So for the next several weeks, she would help her dearest friend, keep herself busy so she didn't stress and anguish over the mess her professional life had become, and hide out from the tabloid journalists who had nothing better to do than stalk a psychologist who liked talking about orgasms. In that respect, Wild Boar Island did sound like a piece of heaven.

At least, until she started to drive across it.

"Have you people never heard of blacktop?" she grumbled as she drove away from the ferry landing, her bones jarring with every bounce of her Prius on the roughly graveled drive.

She'd gotten directions to her rental cottage from her new landlady—whom Callie had put her in touch with—figuring there wasn't much chance of getting lost on this spit of land. Still, nothing was marked and her pampered hybrid was already unhappy.

Her cell phone rang, and she pushed a button on her steering wheel to answer it, using the car's Bluetooth since she had to keep her hands right where they were. It was her friend. "Callie, what have you gotten me into? I'll bet there's not one charging station on this island."

"You'd win that bet. But give it a chance—you'll love it."

"Love" might be an exaggeration, but she would do it because she'd promised Callie. "How are you doing? You sound tired."

"I'm fine. Does any new mother sleep well?" Callie sniffed. "Even one who doesn't have to get up for nightly feedings?"

That sniffle indicated tears, and the comment had revealed a lot about what her friend was feeling. For Callie, not being able to hold her son was probably the second-hardest part of this ordeal—*after* not knowing if he would live or die.

"You'll be doing that soon enough. Right now, rest and get better. You'll need your energy when that sweet boy comes home."

Callie cleared her throat. Lindsey could almost see her petite, curly-haired friend blinking away tears and straightening her shoulders. "So update me. How was the ferry crossing?"

"Hideous. Painful. Awful. This is *not* the heaven you described." Then, wanting to cheer her friend up—and to distract her—she said, "Though, I have to admit, I did meet a man who looked like a male angel. Or, well, maybe hot, sinful devil would be a more appropriate comparison."

Mike, the guy she'd met on the ferry, had been so dark and seductive with all that thick, windblown brown hair; the deep-set, chocolate-brown eyes; square jaw and powerful body. His height had made her feel positively petite, though she stood five-foot-seven. And his mouth was something that should have been carved by an artist. *Pretty* couldn't describe such masculine lips. No, they were… perfect.

No doubt, he'd looked nothing like a safe, innocent seraphim and everything like a wicked, sultry devil sent to seduce women out of their clothes and their good sense. *Yum.*

"Ooooh! Do tell!"

"This superhot, brown-haired guy was on the ferry, too, and he saved my life."

"Did you fall overboard?" Callie squealed.

"Well, no, but I *definitely* considered leaping."

"I understand. It's a lousy mode of transportation. Now spill on this guy. What was his name?"

"Mike."

"Last name?"

"I never got it."

Callie harrumphed. "You so suck at this. Hmm. Mike, brown-haired Adonis? Not ringing a bell. Why didn't you get his full name? Or at least make plans to get together for wild-monkey sex?"

Ahh, Lindsey was glad she'd been able to distract Callie, and that her friend was now feeling better.

"No time. He hurried off the ferry before I had the chance to do either of those things."

Mike had apparently ridden across to the mainland without his car. As soon as they'd docked, he'd gotten a call on his cell phone. His frown as he'd answered said the call was a serious one. Assuring her they'd see each other soon, he'd said goodbye and hurried off the boat, heading toward a big SUV in the parking lot.

Lindsey had been too busy falling to her knees to give thanks for their safe arrival—at least, mentally—to watch him drive away. But during the interminable wait for her car to be unloaded, she'd thought a lot about the handsome stranger.

"Tell me more," Callie ordered. "Gorgeous… What else?"

Her friend knew her well enough to realize Lindsey wouldn't have been fascinated by *just* a handsome face. "He was funny, quick-witted, and had the sexiest smile, complete with dimple."

Realizing she was gushing over a virtual stranger, she fell silent, though she didn't stop mentally ticking off

Mike's attractive qualities. Like his charming protective instincts—he'd assured her he'd dive in after her should she leap overboard, and she believed he'd really meant it. He also had a great, throaty voice and a warm laugh.

Then there were the shoulders. The chest. The powerful arms. Oh lord, the entire package. How could she *not* have noticed his physical appeal, especially once he'd caught her in his arms, holding her safe and steady while her heart lurched far more than the boat had?

And how absolutely crazy that she was so interested in him, considering she had, years ago, built a mental barrier between herself and every man she met?

Sex was fine; she'd have it occasionally, but she never considered how decent a guy was, or if he was protective, or kind. Not having experienced those qualities in many men in her personal life, she'd learned to never look for them. That way she'd never be disappointed when she didn't find them. How strange, then, to find herself realizing that, on the surface at least, this near stranger possessed them all.

"So, he's definitely worthy of the Dr. Smith method, huh? Wait, lemme put on my thinking cap."

Lindsey snickered. Callie was probably the only person who could tease her about the whole mentally inspired-orgasm thing. There'd even been one night at a Mexican restaurant, after a few margaritas, when they'd dared each other to try to think their way into a public climax. But they'd dissolved into giggles almost immediately.

"Definitely Thinkgasm worthy," she replied.

"You know, I bet if you'd researched a man's ability to ejaculate purely by mental fantasy, you'd have gotten a gajillion dollars to fund further study on the subject and a column in *Psychology Today*." Her friend sounded indignant.

"Uh-huh. Instead, I got a *Jeopardy!* question and a meme."

"My mom thought the *Jeopardy!* question was severely cool."

"Well, yeah, it kinda was."

Other than that, though, nothing about her work situation was very cool. Far, far from it. After all her hard work and the passion she had for her field, her research—and now Lindsey herself—was a laughingstock. Which was why it was a very good thing she had something else to do, someone else's problems to focus on. Just hearing Callie's voice had lifted her spirits, and she found herself thankful—again—that she had the other woman for a friend. Knowing how much Callie appreciated her help made it easier for Lindsey to forget about what was going on in the real world. She had work to do on Wild Boar—a new home, a new job, eager students. This would be good for her, very good.

"Anyway, this two-month break should be long enough for the tongues to stop wagging. When I leave here, I'll have hopefully stayed out of the limelight for enough time to get back into my bosses' good graces. I'll be able to reclaim my career and reputation without coming across like the modern-day version of Dr. Ruth."

"Cucumbers…*pfft!* Amateurs," Callie said, with a go-you tone. "Look, I've got to run. Billy's getting out of the shower and we're heading to the hospital."

Wishing her friend a nice day, she hung up and refocused on her driving. She wasn't going to spend any more time thinking about her work problems, any more than she was going to let herself think about sexy Italian-looking dudes with great bodies and killer smiles.

Coming to what she suspected was Wild Boar's main road, she turned right and proceeded toward the south side of the island. There was, Callie had told her, a thriving downtown area to the north. She'd bet the "downtown" consisted of a general store and a total of three restaurants, one of which regularly served a blue-plate special of meat loaf or turkey-and-gravy. She'd save that fun trip for tomorrow since she also needed to find the school where she'd begin teaching on Monday. Right now, though, she just wanted to locate her new home, unpack and lie down to get rid of the lingering seasickness.

Lindsey glanced down at the sheet of paper on which she'd written the landlady's verbal directions, trying to make sense of her own scrawled writing. She was coming to a split in the road, and couldn't tell whether her directions indicated to go right or left…..

"Should've paid attention in Mrs. Dickey's second grade penmanship class," she could hear Callie whispering.

This island wasn't that big. Even if she took a wrong turn, somebody would be able to point her in the correct direction. From what Mike had said, every resident here knew she was coming and where she would be living. Besides, she didn't have a penis; she *was* capable of stopping and asking for directions.

Praying she wasn't making a mistake, she swung to the left at the fork, looking back down at the paper for the name of her next turn. Apparently, though, she spent too much time staring down, because, before she'd even realized anyone was behind her, she heard the quick *blurp-blurp* of a siren.

"Hell," she mumbled, hoping it wasn't a cop and that she wasn't the one being blurped at.

Looking in the rearview mirror, she saw a big, dark vehicle. She noted the spinning dome light on the dash and sighed. Definitely a cop. And right behind her. Blurping.

Wow, her luck was so great lately, she ought to go out and buy a lottery ticket.

Pulling over onto the side of the narrow, unlined road, hoping no big trucks would come by to cream her, she plucked her driver's license out of her wallet, lowered the window and waited.

"What a fantastic way to start my new life," she muttered, rubbing at her eyes with the tips of her fingers. "Can this day get any worse?"

"That depends on how your day's been going so far."

She jerked her hand away from her face, swinging her head to stare at the man standing right beside her car.

The familiar man.

The one who had just kept her from falling overboard into the choppy lake.

The one she'd just been comparing to a heavenly angel *and* a sexy devil.

Mike. Who was, if the lights and siren on his vehicle were to be believed, an officer of the law.

"You have *got* to be kidding me."

"We meet again."

"Please tell me that's a fake light and you're not a real cop."

"Would serial-killer-posing-as-cop-to-lure-unsuspecting-victim work better for you?"

"So not funny."

"Sorry."

She leaned out to gaze up at him, as she wasn't comfortable with the view directly out the driver's-side window. She'd never been more aware of the height of her Prius before now, when she was face-to-crotch with a superhot guy wearing khakis that hugged some of her favorite boy-parts.

"You really are a cop?"

"Chief Mike Santori of the Wild Boar Island P.D., at your service."

Santori. So her Italian speculation had been dead-on. She'd always had such a thing for Italian men. All that dark hair, energy, handsomeness and machismo. *Potent*.

Of course, she rarely got involved with the macho type. Few of them were willing to let a woman call the shots in a relationship. And Lindsey wasn't about to give that up for a well-hung dude with pecs.

There was a second strike against Mike—his niceness. She didn't get involved with men who would expect trust and emotion from her. That way, she wouldn't expect anything like that from them. Safer that way.

He might be worth it.

Perhaps. And if it had *just* been his sex appeal that attracted her, and she hadn't come here to help a friend, she might have given some serious thought to getting to know him better.

She *had*, however, come here to do a job—and to hide out. There was no room in her plan for any man, especially one so unlike the sexy-and-forgettable type she usually went for. Protective, heroic, fun and witty guys weren't the kind of men you could sleep with and forget. Since those were the only men Lindsey would allow herself to get involved with, Mike was definitely off-limits.

Maybe if she kept telling herself that, she'd start to believe it. And maybe she'd stop wondering what it would be like to be touched by those big, strong hands and kissed by that incredible mouth.

Just get through this and drive away.

"Here," she said. Without him asking for it, she thrust her driver's license toward him.

"Lindsey Smith," he said, reading the card aloud, then

handing her back the license, barely glancing at anything else. "I don't think I'll need this."

Hmm. That made it sound as if this wasn't a legitimate traffic stop. Despite her instinctive reaction to him—that he was one of the good guys—annoyance flared within her. Hot and sexy or not, she didn't appreciate people who threw their authority around for their own purposes. But she would give him the benefit of the doubt until she found out what he was really after.

"Were you following me?"

"Not intentionally," he said. "I was told there was an emergency—a missing child—which was why I hurried away from the landing so quickly."

"What happened?"

"It turns out the kid had broken a window playing ball this morning, and was afraid he'd get in trouble. So he was hiding in his own backyard tree house. His mom found him safe and sound right after she called it in."

"That's the best outcome."

"Not for the kid. He's probably going to lose his video games for a month."

Lindsey was glad Mike's mind had gone right to that consequence instead of corporal punishment, which was sort of a hot button for her. Probably not surprising, given her field—she'd certainly dealt with a lot of people traumatized by physical abuse. Still, Mike's comment added to the picture of the kind of person he was. *A good one.* She already knew that much.

Damn, why couldn't she just keep thinking of him as hot? Speculating that he was nice, decent or trustworthy was useless. Though it would almost certainly prevent her from even *considering* giving in to the attraction she felt for him, despite her protestations.

"Anyway, I got the call that he'd been found before I even got to town."

"So were you coming back to the ferry to make sure I hadn't fallen overboard coming down the gangplank?"

"Nope. It was just a coincidence that I spotted this yellow monstrosity in my rearview. I had to remind myself that Big Bird doesn't live here."

She patted her steering wheel. "Don't make fun of her."

"I recognized it, obviously. When I saw which way you were going, I turned around and came after you so I could pull you over."

"Are you allowed to pull me over when you're off duty?"

"What makes you think I'm off duty?"

"You're not in uniform."

A wry grin lifting one corner of his mouth, he slowly unzipped the front of his heavy-duty windbreaker, revealing a buttoned-up, khaki uniform shirt beneath it, complete with a badge on the breast pocket.

"That's not fair. You were practically undercover."

"Were you doing something illegal on the ferry that I missed? Are you a secret Twinkie smuggler or something?"

"Twinkies aren't illegal here, are they?" she asked, feigning horror.

"Not yet, but there is a new eat-healthy initiative at the school."

"I'll be sure to stock up, like those Doomsday Preppers did when the world thought Twinkies would be gone forever."

"Good plan. Now, Lindsey Smith, why don't you tell me why you were so worried about me pulling you over?"

Yeah. Why *was* she worried? She hadn't been speeding—heaven knew it would be hard to get her car up to

any speed on these roads. So why had he pulled her over...
just because he wanted to see her again?

Even as she reminded herself she didn't like these tactics, a thrill of excitement raced through her. There'd definitely been attraction between them; she knew he'd felt it,
too. She hadn't for one second *really* believed he was gay.

Maybe his spiel about not being interested in women
or relationships had been a cover, just a line to keep from
seeming too interested. Maybe he'd recognized her car
and followed a crazy impulse, stopping her so he could
ask her to meet him for a drink, or a pleasant walk along
the beach, or for hot, steamy sex in the nearest bed.

Cool it.

Whatever the reason, she forced herself to remember
she wasn't interested. Okay, she *was* interested—definitely
aware of him, as any woman would be aware of a guy so
hot he should come with a warning label and oven mitts.
But, aside from already having decided he was *so* not her
type, she, for one, had meant it when she said she wasn't
on Wild Boar for romance, or sex. Those were the last two
complications she needed to add to her life. Lying low and
hoping people forgot about her supposed obsession with
orgasms wouldn't be easy if the local police chief started
giving her lots of orgasms. Although, she had to admit, it
would certainly be fun.

"I'm not worried," she finally replied, forcing orgasms
out of her head. She'd work on her own think-method later,
when she was alone. "I'm just surprised you didn't mention your status as the island's chief enforcer."

"That makes me sound like a mobster, not a cop."

"Sorry. Now, come on, tell me why you pulled me over.
Could you just not resist following me?" she asked, flirting
a little, despite her own best interest and good intentions.

He admitted it, slowly nodding. "You got me. I had to come after you. I couldn't help myself."

She swallowed hard, wishing she hadn't started something she knew she couldn't finish. Flirtation was fun— she usually enjoyed it, especially with a guy as attractive as this one. But she was here to lie low, not to *get* laid.

But she just couldn't resist. "It's the hair, isn't it?" she asked with a feigned sigh. "Yes, it's my natural color."

He bent down so he was squatting beside the car, resting a forearm on the door. They were practically face-to-face now, and the position gave her the chance to study those dark, dreamy eyes, framed by the thickest, longest lashes she'd ever seen on a man.

He watched her just as intently, answering, "It's not the hair, but thanks for clarifying. It's not your pretty eyes, either."

She licked her lips, enjoying the way his stare roved over her face, as if he not only liked what he saw, but was memorizing her features to think about later. Hmm.

"Well?"

"Two things. First, you have my gloves."

His gloves. Damn, she'd totally forgotten to give them back, had simply stuffed them into the pockets of her raincoat. She flushed, immediately grabbing them and shoving them toward him. "I'm so sorry. I was just so relieved to get off that ferry I wasn't thinking clearly."

"Don't worry about it. I'm the one who raced off for the near-emergency."

He took the gloves from her, his fingertips brushing against hers, lightly, softly, and he didn't immediately pull away. She sucked in a surprised breath at the excitement she felt at such simple skin-to-skin contact. They'd been mashed together, full-frontal, during their choppy boat ride, but through the bulk of their clothes and coats, she hadn't been able to register much more than a quick acknowledgment that he felt as strong and powerful as he looked. This brief, innocent connection of fingertips somehow seemed more intimate. Quick pictures flashed through her head of those strong, warm hands touching lots of other places on her body.

Lindsey was a big advocate of women taking care of themselves, being in complete control—financially, emotionally, physically and sexually. But oh, lord, did she love big, strong, man-hands.

"What's the second reason?" she whispered, not sure whether she wanted him to say she'd forgotten something on the boat, or that he wanted to take her out for a blue-plate special.

Meat loaf's good. I like meat loaf.

"Well, there's also the fact that…"

"Yes?"

"You're going the wrong direction down a one-way street."

3

"SHUT UP!"

Mike wasn't sure what Lindsey had expected him to say—that she'd grabbed his interest along with his gloves? That he'd wanted to see her again? That he'd be happy to show her around?

All that was true. But, remembering their conversation on the trip over, he knew better than to say it. Neither of them was in the market. She was a schoolteacher, for heaven's sake, and he was the chief of police. They couldn't afford the kind of gossip that would arise if the two newcomers, both in respectable positions, hooked up.

That was especially true for him, considering his very job might be on the line. If the town council decided he was spending too much time romancing a woman when he should be focused on his probationary period, he might not have a job to stick with. He needed to keep reminding himself of that, no matter how much he found himself thinking about those sparkling green eyes or that stunning red hair.

Her goggle-eyed expression and gut response almost made him laugh, but he clarified, "Uh, me shutting up won't change the fact that you're going the wrong way."

"You're serious?"

"Serious as an IRS audit." He jerked a thumb toward the fork in the road, at which she'd taken a decidedly wrong turn. "The road switches from two to one-way at the split. It single-lanes in a long loop around the base of the island."

She continued to gape and sputter. "Is there a *sign?*"

"Yup."

"I can't believe I missed it." She shifted in her seat, peering out through the misty morning air, looking for the road sign, then let out an audible sigh when she spotted it. "I'm very sorry—I'm usually a good driver. I was trying to read my own lousy handwriting for the directions and wasn't paying close enough attention."

She showed him a sheet of paper on which was scrawled something that might have been English, but also might have been a secret code used by the Allies in World War II.

"Wow. You write more like a doctor than a schoolteacher."

She bit her bottom lip.

"I thought all teachers had good penmanship."

"I'm not exactly a typical teacher."

That was an understatement. If any of his science teachers had been as sexy as her, he may have ended up a Nobel Prize–winning biochemist. "You're sure not like any of the ones I had."

"To be fair, you're not exactly how I'd pictured the chief of police of a remote island to look."

"What would you expect?"

"Umm… A sixty-five-year-old with gray hair and a fishing pole?"

"You just described the guy I replaced," he admitted. "But I don't have the patience for fishing. I'm more of a pickup-basketball fan myself."

"So, Kobe, is there a lot of call for police chiefing here on the island?"

"We have our fair share of crime, you know."

"Hotbed of criminal activity, is it?"

"Some gang stuff going on." Her eyes nearly popped out of her head. Chuckling, he added, "A gang of nine-year-olds went into the general store and swiped candy bars on a dare."

"I take it they weren't armed?"

"Only with loud whines and lots of crocodile tears when they got caught."

"Did you arrest them?"

"Nah, I let them off with a warning. Their parents were so mad, I have no doubt those kids won't do it again."

"What about me? Are you going to let me off with a warning, or are you going to give me a ticket?"

"Trying to decide. Should I cite you for going the wrong way, stealing my gloves or telling an officer of the law to shut up?"

She must have recognized the teasing note in his voice, because a soft laugh gurgled from her mouth. "Sorry about that."

"S'okay. You might have been trying to decipher your messy writing, but the truth is, the sign's also a bit hidden by some overgrown bushes." She glanced back again, and he did, too, barely making out the sign. He hadn't been exaggerating. "I'll get somebody from the town maintenance crew to come out and trim the bushes. I guess the crew's not prepared for newcomers who don't know their way around so early in the spring."

"Thanks, though I should have seen it, even if the underbrush is a bit overgrown."

"Let me hit the lights and siren and turn you around so you don't get beaned by a truck while you get to the correct side of the loop. Then I'll lead you to your new home."

He wondered if she would argue, but she must have still

been light-headed from her water voyage since she didn't. That was good. Not only because the roads were twisty and, in some cases, made no sense, but also because of the possible condition of her cottage. He didn't know Lindsey well, but he sure didn't want to think about her walking in the door and getting a faceful of spiderweb or a lungful of dusty air.

Jogging back to his SUV, he switched on the siren and light again then swung around, watching as she did the same. He led her the short distance to the fork, turned down the correct side and easily found his way to her new place. He had only lived on Wild Boar for a few months, but he was already familiar with just about every inch of it. There weren't very many inches, after all.

Pulling up in front of the old Wymer place, which was now empty since the elderly owner had moved in with her equally elderly, also-widowed sister in town, he drove around to the small cottage in the back of the property. The sisters clearly hadn't given much thought to the condition of the place. Weeds choked the front garden, and the small fence lining the cobbled walkway sagged, as if on the verge of collapse. Paint was peeling off the cottage's siding, and the front door was pitted and sorely in need of a coat of wood stain.

Lindsey pulled up next to him and got out of her car, her shoulders slumping as she eyed what would be her home for the next couple of months. "Well, it's not exactly as I pictured it."

"Couldn't you stay at your friend's house while she's gone? Isn't she staying somewhere near the hospital on the mainland close to her baby?"

"Yes, but her husband works here, and he'll be at home most work nights. I barely know him. It would be really awkward."

That did pose a problem.

"Maybe it's not so bad inside," she said.

He heard a note of optimism in her voice and didn't have the heart to disagree. Hoping she was right, he pushed open the creaky gate and walked up onto the porch, the boards of which sank beneath his feet with every step. "Dry rot," he said. "Be careful coming in and out of this place."

She nodded. "Mrs. Wymer said the key is under the mat."

"Let's hope that part of the porch hasn't collapsed and the mat's not covering a giant hole," he said, bending to check. Fortunately, the flooring was still intact and the key was in place. Retrieving it, he rose and unlocked the door. "Why don't you let me go in first? I can't say for sure there are wild animals in there, but I wouldn't be surprised if a raccoon or some squirrels had made a home out of your cottage."

"Oh, God, when does that ferry leave again?" she mumbled.

Considering that by the end of their journey, she'd appeared ready to drop to her knees and kiss dry land, she, too, must be very concerned about what they would find behind the locked door.

Fortunately, though, they were both wrong. Because, while Mrs. Wymer might not have been able to do anything about the outside, as soon as he pushed open the cottage door, he realized the inside had been cleaned and freshened. The air smelled of pine and the wood floors gleamed. The cushions on an old-fashioned sofa had been plumped, and fresh flowers sat on a coffee table in front of it.

"Thank heaven," Lindsey said as she walked in, a smile breaking over her face as she looked around her new home.

There wasn't much to see, and he could glimpse almost all of it from right where he stood. The front door opened into a decent-size living room. To the left was a small kitchen, and through a door to the right he spied a bedroom with, he had to note, a nice-size bed.

Don't think about her bed. Mentally going down that road with this sexy woman would lead only to frustration and a need to get reacquainted with his hand.

"You really had me scared for a minute," said Lindsey.

"I was scared myself. She must have hired somebody to come out and get things ready for you."

Lindsey was crossing to the kitchen table, where a plastic-wrapped plate of cookies sat, decorated with a bow and a card. She opened it. "Yes, this says that's exactly what she did."

"Excellent."

"Oh, I needed this so much I think I'll offer her a kidney if she ever wants one. She says she left coffee, sugar and creamer, too!" She immediately turned toward the pantry, opening it and cooing when she spied a can of dark grounds.

Without waiting for an invitation, he went over to the coffeemaker and began to fill the pot with water from the tap. The two of them worked together, falling into a routine that was as normal as it was unexpected. They just... synced.

After the coffee was brewed, she poured him a cup without even asking if he wanted one. He took it, added some milk then joined her at the small kitchen table. She sipped at her mug, closing her eyes and sighing with pleasure.

Man, he liked how she looked when she was enjoying herself. Of course, he'd also liked how she looked on that boat, when she had not been enjoying herself.

"Want a cookie?" she asked.

Mrs. Wymer hadn't been among those who'd offered

him baked goodies, but he wasn't about to refuse a home-made chocolate chip. He helped himself. Lindsey did not take one, still a bit green around the gills and content with her coffee.

"I should probably warn you," he said, "this part of the island is really deserted this time of year. You won't be having any neighbors stop by to borrow a cup of sugar."

"I noticed." A tiny frown line appeared between her eyes. "I never had neighbors borrowing sugar before, but this quiet will still really take some getting used to."

"No doubt about it. I live right downtown and I still haven't gotten used to how sleepy it is, even there. It's just a different lifestyle compared to anywhere on the mainland."

"What about the rest of the lifestyle? Have you gotten used to that?"

He wished he could reassure her, but he really couldn't. "I think if you weren't born here, it's very hard not to feel like an outsider."

"Cliquishness?"

"Not really," he said, remembering all the offers he'd gotten from his new neighbors and colleagues. "The people are friendly…it's just there's a lack of common ground. Islanders have different outlooks, backgrounds, experiences."

"Sounds a little lonely."

He sipped his coffee, considering her observation, and then nodded. "I guess it is, but maybe that's my own fault. I'm just out of step with the locals."

"I feel a little out of step with people no matter where I am," she admitted, gazing at the dark, steaming liquid in her cup.

She sounded as though she was speaking more to herself than to him. Interesting that a woman this attractive didn't feel like she fit in anywhere.

"You'd think with all this loneliness, you'd at least get some privacy here," he said with a smile, trying to lighten the mood. "But you can kiss that goodbye. You might not have people peeking into your windows, but they'll be commenting on your every move once you get a mile from home."

"Oh, joy. You make this sound so appealing, I can't imagine why it took me almost thirty years to move here."

"I'm sure you'll survive for two months."

She stared at him directly. "Will you survive forever?"

Mike rubbed his jaw, not answering immediately. He thought about what had driven him here; he couldn't go back to that way of life. Finally he said, "I don't know about forever, but I'm hoping for a few years, anyway."

"Well, then I hope it works out for you."

Mike lingered to talk for a while longer. He gave her directions to town, told her where the school was, and about the difficult parking situation there. He also warned her which specials to avoid at the most popular diner in town, and enjoyed how her soft laughter rolled over him.

After he'd finished, he stood up, taking the cup to the sink and rinsing it out. "Guess I should leave you to it."

Rising as well, she said, "Thank you so much for helping me get here. I appreciate you not giving me a ticket."

Lindsey led him toward the door, pushing a slight smile to her lips, but he noticed the slump of her shoulders and knew she wasn't totally ready to be alone. He understood what she was feeling. Coming here, so far away from everything that was familiar, had been tough for him, too. But Lindsey was not only in a new home, in a new job, she was also extremely worried about her friend—every word she'd said about Callie Parker and her infant son revealed that.

He should go. He'd left the island a little after dawn,

hadn't even been in to the office yet. For all he knew, there'd been an armed robbery of the Main Street Bank, or worse. Maybe one of his officers—like Ollie Dickinson, who resembled Gaston from *Beauty and the Beast,* and shared his temperament and brain power—had taken over his office. Ollie had been on the force for a couple of years and had fully expected to get the job Mike had "stolen." The man hadn't exactly been friendly to Mike.

But Mike wasn't ready to leave Lindsey, and it had nothing to do with the fact that she suddenly looked a little like a sad, lonely waif. For a few minutes there, when they'd sat at the table, sharing coffee and conversation, she'd perked up, brightened, even laughed. Now…well, he hated to see her seem so weary. Part of him wanted to pull her in his arms and hug her, convince her it would be all right, that she hadn't moved to the ass end of nowhere.

Well, she *had* moved to the ass end of nowhere, but honestly, it wasn't *that* bad.

Barring a hug, though—and he was barring that—spending more time with her proved irresistible. What harm was there in lending a little moral support to a newcomer who was just as much a fish out of water as he'd been when he'd moved here? Hell, he *still* was that way.

Whatever Ollie had done to his office, even if he had to undo legal damage…it was worth it to be with her a little longer.

"Did you bring all your stuff in your car?" he asked.

"Yes. Since the place was described as furnished, I only packed clothes, my laptop and some personal things. Oh, and books. If I'm going to be teaching science, I'll need to brush up."

"Why don't I help you bring it in? From what I remember of science books, they weigh a ton."

"You really don't have to do that."

He waved off her objections, already turning to head out the front door. Reaching her car, he spied some boxes on the backseat, and bent to hoist one. Lindsey, sensibly—he liked that—didn't argue further, instead just opening the trunk and grabbing things, too.

As she'd said, she hadn't brought a lot with her. A couple of suitcases, a laptop and printer, some sheets and towels—he could understand wanting those around her to give her a sense of home.

Then there were the books.

"Damn, you said 'books,' you didn't say 'library,'" he said as he hefted a fourth heavy carton out of the trunk and carried it into the cottage. "You planning to teach the kindergartners about quantum physics?"

She shrugged, walking over to place her own box on the floor beside a table in the living room. The table was already covered with the first few they'd brought in. He had no idea where she intended to put all the books; the place certainly didn't have an office. Or bookshelves. Or much more floor space.

"I want to do some work on my own project while I'm here."

She didn't elaborate and he didn't question her. Instead, he went back outside to bring in the last container—a laundry basket containing detergents and cleaning supplies. When he returned, he said, "Were you a Girl Scout? You came prepared."

"Definitely not a Scout," she said with a twist of her mouth. "You had to pay money to join the Scouts, and no way would my parents have ever done that for me."

He frowned, hearing a jaded sadness in her voice. Obviously she had some issues with her folks.

Having been raised by loving, generous parents, who had given him and his brothers as much as they could afford to give, he really couldn't imagine growing up that way. But it wasn't exactly a conversation for the first day they'd met.

"I'm just glad I don't have to start using those cleaning products right away," she said, pushing a few long strands of hair away from her face. She yawned broadly. "I could really use a nap."

"It's the seasickness. But you should probably have a decent meal before you lie down."

She grimaced. "Even if I wanted to, that would be tough. I've got Mrs. Wymer's cookies and, I think, some mints in my purse. That's about it."

"No Twinkies?" he asked with wag of his brows.

Remembering their earlier conversation, she smiled. "I'm afraid not."

"There's always a diner."

"If the Saturday lunch special is meat loaf, I'd consider it," she said with another yawn as she put one more box on top of the others on the table. "Otherwise, I'm taking a nap."

"Understood." He turned to leave, realizing there was no sense in delaying things further, especially since she obviously just wanted to sleep.

Right before he reached the door, he glanced back and saw the precarious pile of boxes had reached critical mass. It had been leaning before. Now, with the one she'd just placed there, the whole thing was teetering. Watching him, she hadn't even noticed.

"Look out!"

He lunged toward her, noting her start of surprise, but ignoring it. Diving just beyond her, he stopped the entire stack from toppling down, though he was unable to prevent the very top box from sliding to its death. It hit the floor hard, the tape splitting and the flaps popping open.

Books and other items spewed out, clattering onto the hardwood floor. The books stopped where they fell, but the other things spun around, one skittering all the way across the room.

"You almost got clobbered," he said.

She did not reply; in fact, she didn't even look at him. She was too busy staring at the items that had spilled out of the box. Lindsey stood as still as a statue, her already pale face losing its last little bit of color. "Oh, my God."

He followed her stare, wondering what had her so frazzled. At first, he just saw random books and some hard-plastic-wrapped, oddly shaped packages that didn't quite register. Then he stepped closer and bent down.

The title of one of the books flashed across his consciousness: *Giving Yourself Ultimate Pleasure.* On the cover was a woman, her head thrown back, mouth open on a sensual moan, one hand covering her bare breasts, the other between her legs.

Shocked, he froze in place. His heart leaped up into the vicinity of his throat. All the sexual energy and base attraction he'd felt for Lindsey since he'd spied her on that ferry gushed through him. And that was before he got a better look at some of those oddly shaped items and realized what they all had in common.

When it sank in what he was seeing, Mike grabbed for the back of the nearest chair. Trying to stay steady on suddenly wobbly legs, he exclaimed, "Wild Boar Island's new schoolteacher is a sex addict."

"I am *not* a sex addict," Lindsey said, sounding torn between indignation and utter dismay.

"Sorry," Mike said, acknowledging as soon as the words had left his mouth that they should have stayed in his head.

But, *damn.* The woman had packed like she meant business—sexy business for one—which was enough to make a man cry. Just from where he stood, he spied at least a dozen female-oriented sex toys, including a pink butterfly thing that the package claimed was to be "strapped on." A small purple one, shaped like a tiny porpoise, appeared designed to clip onto a woman's finger. There was a small, metal case for storing what might pass for marbles on a playground but were identified as Ben Wa balls instead.

But wait, there's more.

He spied several slim vibrators in various colors and textures. And a black harness-looking thing that didn't seem as if it was made for a single player, which just made his breath grow that much thicker in his lungs. He saw the box for another device called an "anal probe," which to him sounded like an alien torture tool.

Then his wide-eyed stare fell on the thick, long, extremely graphic-looking device that wasn't quite as big as what he had in his pants but was pretty damned generous nonetheless. It was not plastic-wrapped. Nor was the one beside it—little dong's giant brother. The thing was big enough to hold a lamp shade.

Holy shit.

He couldn't move. Literally, could not lift a hand, or take a step or do anything except stare. Most of the sex aids were still in their packaging, but he couldn't stop himself from wondering if she'd ever opened, used and then repackaged any of them. Or if, God help him, she'd used the ones that *weren't* still packaged, like the huge dildo.

He didn't imagine any woman could take that massive conversation piece into herself…but the other one… Had she plunged it into her body? If he bent down and picked it up, would he be able to tell? Did it still hold a faint whiff of musky woman? And Christ, why did he so desperately want to *do* things to her with it?

Wild, erotic images flooded his brain, saturating his

imagination. More than just fucking her with that long ridge of rubber, he could close his eyes and picture Lindsey giving herself pleasure, just like the woman on the book. It took no effort at all to imagine her clipping that tiny, purple device onto her finger and sliding it between her thighs, letting the vibrating tip brush against her clit until her hips thrust in sheer need. Her other hand would be on her breast, stroking, squeezing, gently plucking at a perfect nipple as the intensity increased. When she came, she'd be dying for something thick and hard to fill her, and no rubber toy could possibly give her the heat she craved.

But he could. Oh, hell, yes, he could.

In fact, he could practically do it right now. Those mental images were causing stabbing sensations in his groin, and he thought he might burst his zipper.

God help me.

He shook his head, chasing all those pictures out of his mind. He knew they would creep back in later, when he was alone in his small house. It had, after all, been a while since he'd had sex. The last time had been with his upward-climbing ex, before he'd moved here. But, blue balls or not, he sure didn't want to come across as some horny asshole taking advantage of an admittedly *unusual* situation.

"Sorry, I seem to have dropped your lifetime supply of vibrators," he finally said, wondering how on earth he could sound so calm when he was certain he hadn't breathed for the past several seconds.

She groaned. "I can explain."

"Not necessary. You obviously own stock in a sex toy company?"

She dropped her face into her hands, shaking her head. "Please be gone before I open my eyes again," she said, sounding beyond embarrassed, verging on humiliated.

He cursed himself for being so flippant. She had to be

mortified. He sure would have been if a stranger had gotten
a look at his most intimate reading material and personal
items. Not that he usually *read* what was between the pages
of his subscription mags, the ones delivered in a discreet,
brown wrapper. Plus, of course, he also didn't subscribe
to a pocket-pussy-of-the-month club, so there wouldn't be
anything equivalent to shock the average passerby

When he combined the book with the toys, it was obvious this woman took that whole giving-yourself-pleasure
thing to heart. Which just made him wonder what it might
be like to take that chore from her pretty, soft hands.

Swallowing hard, he said, "Look, don't be embarrassed.
It's no big deal." Trying to pretend he hadn't been imag-
ining her putting something thick and hard between her
thighs, he scrambled for another explanation. "It's, uh, not
as if I believe you're opening an X-rated shop on the island." Frowning, he added, "You're not, are you?"

"Of course not. I don't imagine there would be much
call for that around here."

"You might be surprised," he said, thinking of a few
people who seriously needed to have something shoved up
their ass. One of them was Ollie, his own officer, a subordinate who hadn't yet learned the meaning of that word—
subordinate. The guy was a buffoon, a good ole' boy who
never would have made it on the force in any mainland
city. Apparently, he'd made it on this one only by virtue
of being the former chief's nephew.

"Besides," she said with a definite eye roll, "that *wasn't*
what I imagined you were thinking."

No. She probably imagined he was thinking about how
she used all these wickedly sexual items on her own stunning, curvy body. Which, of course, he had been.

He met her stare, silently admitting it. She held that
stare, from sheer bravado or because she, too, had suddenly

started envisioning all-too-sexy ideas about the interesting things two people could get up to with all those appliances.

He'd had a few relationships and more than his share of brief flings. But he honestly couldn't remember if he'd ever progressed to *this* level of intimacy before. Frankly, he'd never understood why any guy would want to when he had his own hands, mouth and cock to work with.

Just glancing at the colorful items strewn across the floor, however, and picturing running the tip of a slender vibrator over all the most sensitive parts of her body, was enough to open up his mind. He totally got off on oral sex—but how much better might it be if he filled her with a sexy, vibrating toy while he pleasured her with his tongue? Even that alien-probing toy suddenly sounded a little more interesting. He could see how a woman might be interested in double penetration without having to go to bed with two men.

Da-yum.

Forget it. Not double, not even single.

They weren't just two people who could get up to sexy games; they were strangers. Two strangers who couldn't get involved, no matter what.

Because if they so much as *touched* one of those kinky things at the same time, he feared the news would smash into the island's *grapevine* so fast everybody would be drinking Merlot by nightfall.

"Then again, I do like wine," he mumbled under his breath. Hell, Chianti might as well have been in his bottle as a baby, it was such a part of Santori tradition.

Her brow shot up. "What?"

"Talking to myself. I'm a little out of my element with this one."

"That makes two of us." She shook her head, nibbled her lip, then leaned down to begin picking up the strewn items.

Knowing better than to pick up any of the naughtier things for her, he went for the giving-yourself-pleasure book. Unable to resist, he turned it over and read the description on the back. It hinted that the pages contained all kinds of secrets and tips on how a woman could achieve ultimate satisfaction, sans man.

"You don't really *need* this, do you?" he found himself asking, not sure where the question had come from, or why he'd voiced it. His common sense, and tact, seemed to have departed when it came to Lindsey Smith, some inner bad boy making him up the stakes, just a little.

She'd been grabbing sex toys and shoving them into the box, but stopped midway to stare at him before replying to his question. He tried not to look at the Jolly Green Giant–size dong she was holding and instead focused only on her face.

"What do you mean?"

He could blow it off, retreat to safe conversational territory—if there was such a thing, considering she was holding a two-foot-long cock and he a manual on masturbation. But something made him persist. "You're beautiful. You're sexy as hell. Why would you need to…"

"Have sex by myself?"

"Something along those lines."

Her lashes fluttered; she glanced away, twisting the phallus in her hands as if she didn't even realize she was holding it. He flinched, unable to help it, because, while the idea of having those slim fingers wrapped around his own dick was exciting as hell, he didn't think he'd be up for that much hand-wringing. Mr. Big Dong didn't seem to mind, though; those sex-toy makers obviously made their products very sturdy.

"Maybe I just don't believe in having to rely on anyone

else, sexually or otherwise. Some women like having all the control in their hands."

Her hands? He managed not to smirk at that line, even though she'd practically begged for a smirk.

"I mean," she said, apparently noticing his expression, "they might prefer to be in the driver's seat."

That one he couldn't resist. "You'd have to be one hell of a driver to handle *that* stick."

A tiny smile flitted across her mouth. "I guess. But the truth is...these things aren't really mine."

He grimaced. "They're borrowed?"

"I meant, I didn't buy them," she said with an eye roll.

"Did you knock over that big-name sex shop, Bare Essentials, before you left Chicago?"

"Of course not. They're samples. They were for research."

"Are you preparing for your entry into the adult-film business?"

"Hardly."

"That's good, because I'm fairly sure the 'hot for teacher' story has already been done. About a million times."

"How many versions have you seen?" she asked, her expression unchanged, though her voice held the tiniest bit of suggestion.

"Maybe a few."

Her wicked smile made Mike realize he wasn't the only one giving in to some naughty urges here. She, too, was pushing this, even though the safe, sane thing would have been to let the conversation drop along with the dildo.

He stepped closer, pausing only to let the book fall into the open box at his feet. She didn't move away, tossing her own retrieved item in there, as well. It landed with a thud.

"You could kill someone with that thing," he mused.

"Maybe I should keep it handy to slam into any potential intruders."

He rubbed his jaw. Damn, the woman did know how to give a guy an opening. But those green eyes didn't reveal whether she'd done it on purpose. "Slam it, huh?"

Her eyes flared, even as she inched a little closer, too. "I didn't mean to say that."

"I'm sure you didn't." He watched her mouth as her tongue flicked out to dampen her parted lips. She was breathing deeply, audibly. But then, so was he. "Maybe you meant to say pound, or thrust?"

She swallowed visibly, that delicate throat bobbing. "I meant, I could use it as a weapon."

"Yeah, I'm sure that'd scare a home invader to death. Go away or I'll beat you with my big, giant penis."

Her dark pupils widened and her eyes flared with excitement, as if she'd felt the electric thrill in the air. Hell, so had he. He'd felt it from the moment he'd seen her on the deck of that ferry this morning.

"This is a dangerous conversation, Chief Santori," she whispered, even as she wrapped her arms around herself, as if for warmth. Or to hide any evidence of her body's reaction to that dangerous conversation. Because he hadn't been able to help noticing that her nipples were pebbled beneath her soft sweater and a pretty flush had risen in her previously pale cheeks.

"I'm not intimidated by your sex toy, teacher," he said, his voice almost a purr. His turn to give the opening; he just wondered if she'd take it.

Her chin went up. "Should I be intimidated by yours?"

Oh, hell, the woman hadn't just taken it, she'd twisted his words around and put him firmly on the defensive. His mouth went dry, his hand shook and his whole body strained to eliminate those last few inches that separated them. He wanted to kiss her, wanted to push her up against the wall and cover her mouth with his, to taste her and *take* her.

It was madness. She was a stranger, they were both firmly opposed to any kind of sexual entanglements and he was in a new job in a place where the walls had eyes and ears.

And yet. *And yet...*

One kiss. One simple taste. Who would it harm?

He reached for her, cupping her cheek, tugging her toward him. He didn't try to overpower her, letting her duck away if she chose to.

But she didn't. Instead, she stepped into him, throwing her arms around his neck and rising on tiptoe to take the kiss he'd been about to offer her. Her soft lips melded against his, and parted. Mike groaned, taking what she gave him, sliding his tongue against hers, exploring that sweet-tasting mouth.

He liked kissing. He'd missed kissing. And kissing this particular woman could easily become an addiction.

Every inch of her womanly body was pressed against him, from the softness of her mouth, the lushness of her perfect breasts, the flat tummy, the curvy hips, the long legs. This wasn't some sweet, exploring first kiss; it was a hot and hungry stolen interlude. One both of them knew wasn't going to last and shouldn't be repeated, so they would have to make the most of it.

He angled his head one way and she angled hers the other so their tongues could plunge deeper. Her fingers twined in his hair, his dropped to her hips and they pressed into each other, making no effort to pretend they weren't both incredibly turned on.

He was turned on. But not crazy. Certainly not crazy enough to have sex with a woman he'd met four hours ago.

Especially not one who was his new neighbor, and the trusted new schoolteacher for the island's kids.

It almost killed him, but he let common sense invade, and slowly, he ended the kiss. He didn't pull away completely, keeping his mouth near hers so they could share each deep, gasping breath. He didn't release her hips, and she still had a death grip on his hair. He sensed she was fighting the same inner battle as him, knowing it was time to end this, but almost pained at having to do the smart thing.

But finally, he did the smart thing. He dropped his hands and took a step back.

"I'd better go," he said, shaking off the crazy desire to pick her up, carry her into her new room and see just how bouncy the bedsprings were in her big bed.

"Yes," she murmured, lifting a hand to her mouth and brushing her fingertips across her swollen, reddened lips. "That would be for the best."

"Should I apologize?"

"I wish you wouldn't."

He nodded then strode toward the door, focused only on getting out of here before this situation could get any crazier. Unfortunately, his feet didn't get the message that they were to avoid anything suggestive. With his second step, he accidentally kicked the more normal-size, veiny-looking toy, sending it spinning like the world's most salacious dreidel.

He paused, watching it disappear under the couch. She did, too. Then it was gone, the squeak of rubber on hardwood ended, leaving them in thick silence. She opened her mouth to say something—*hey, watch what you're doing with my favorite toy?*

But he threw a hand up, palm out, stopping her. He couldn't stand here another minute thinking about what had fallen out of her box, or the fact that it had led to a wild, impulsive kiss that was going to live in his dreams and his memories for the rest of his life.

Nor could he think about why Lindsey Smith, the new science teacher of a quaintly old-fashioned public school, traveled with a vast array of naughty pleasure devices. Or why he, the new Chief of Police, had kissed her like he needed the air in her lungs to survive. Or why they'd met here, now, when neither of them was in a position to do anything about the intense attraction they were both experiencing. He simply moved past her, not saying another word, walking out the door, shutting it with hard finality behind him.

Her thoughts were apparently just as wild and scattered as his own. Before he even stepped off the porch, he heard a loud, feminine groan coming from inside the house. If he had to guess, he'd call it frustration mixed with embarrassment.

He didn't pause, didn't even consider turning back; he simply strode toward his SUV. As he got in and started it up, he found himself hoping that, by the time he saw her again, he'd have stopped thinking about how she'd tasted, how she'd felt in his arms.

And how much he wanted to get a crash course in the use of X-rated toys.

4

AFTER WATCHING MIKE SANTORI drive away, Lindsey spent about twenty minutes being mortified, and not just about the whole sex-toys-on-the-floor moment. There was also the fact that she'd kissed a complete stranger like she intended to swallow his tongue.

She was a professional. She taught people how to deal with their sexual urges, and counseled women on how to respect their bodies and choose their partners. She'd made her own sexual choices with deliberation and caution, always aware of exactly the kind of man she was choosing and why she was choosing him.

Yet she had made out with Mike like she was a horny cheerleader and he the high school stud who could snap his fingers and have any girl in the school.

"Not this girl," she reminded herself. "That will never happen again, and don't you forget it."

Reminding herself of that over and over, she finished packing up her…research tools. Because, despite what he might have imagined, all those ridiculous-looking toys that had been strewn across her floor *were* strictly for research.

She was a sex therapist, for heaven's sake. She counseled women on taking control of their sexuality. Of course companies tried to get her to recommend their products.

Plus, when she'd been working on her dissertation, Lindsey had not only interviewed dozens of women, she had also examined just about every sexual aid on the market. Companies had happily sent her samples of their products, and if Chief Santori thought he'd seen the bulk of her collection, he had another think coming. She had loads more stored in her spare room in her Chicago apartment. That's where that particular box should have remained. Either she or the doorman she'd paid to help her move must have grabbed it by mistake.

Still a little stunned about what had happened, she carried the now-repacked box to the closet and shoved it in the rear corner. She was determined to get it back to the mainland the very first chance she got, even if it meant going over on that stupid ferry again.

The only thing she'd salvaged from the box before she'd sealed it were a few textbooks and a small, pocket-size illustrated edition of the Kama Sutra. It had been a gift from Callie, who'd said when she'd given it to her that Lindsey needed to learn the concept of intimacy.

She'd been offended at the time. She'd been intimate with people—with men. But even though she'd told her friend she was being ridiculous, she recognized something in Callie's words.

She had sex. She didn't do intimacy. Intimacy—real intimacy—required trust, commitment and letting go. It meant opening yourself up and being vulnerable. It required you to be willing to be hurt by someone.

Those were the lessons she tried to teach her patients. But she hadn't taught them to herself.

Because she'd had enough of being vulnerable in her life. She'd seen what it could lead to, had lived it and taken notes throughout her childhood with parents who put the funk in dysfunctional. They'd despised and derided each other when they were together, and then longed for each other when they were apart. *Obsessive* didn't describe their psychologically abusive relationship, and Lindsey had been the innocent bystander who'd had to watch them live it.

No way was she going down that road as an adult. She'd rather be alone, completely alone, than to love/hate another person so much it drove her to madness.

Callie knew about Lindsey's cautious approach to relationships and sex. Sure, Lindsey'd had sex, with several men. But none had ever made her want to try the Push-cart position, much less the Trapeze. Because that kind of sex required serious trust and intimacy. And that just wasn't how Lindsey rolled.

Until Mike?

"Forget it," she mumbled aloud, tempted to go back to the closet, tear the fresh tape off that box and stuff the pretty, colorful little book inside it. There was certainly no chance it would be put to use while she was living on Wild Boar Island...even if she *could* close her eyes and lose herself in the memory of Mike Santori's kisses. One embrace had convinced her that the man knew how to drive a woman wild.

"No being wild," she reminded herself. She simply couldn't afford to be. She had to be quiet, and live a boring, spotless life, free from any hint of sexiness that might give her detractors more to laugh about, or meme her over. She wanted her job back, damn it, which meant keeping her nose clean so Big Brother Dr. Ross and his buddies had nothing to hold against her.

No wildness. No risk. No loss of control. And no possibility of opening herself up to hurt, she decided as she crawled into bed.

That didn't, of course, stop her from having the kind of dreams that pushed her into an orgasm in her sleep that night.

She came so hard she was rocked into full wakefulness at dawn Sunday morning, even though she hadn't slept well in the unfamiliar bed. And the rumbles and quakes roaring through her body, the sizzling heat, the heightened sensitivity of all her nerve endings, told her she hadn't dreamed the climax, she'd actually had one.

It wasn't the first time. The whole concept of climaxing in a dream—something that had been happening to her since her teen years—had been what had prompted her doctoral research. If the mind really was the pleasure center for a woman, so that merely *dreaming* could bring orgasm, why couldn't women do it while awake?

Answer: they could. A little research had proved that, and a lot of research had gone on to explain why.

The part of herself that always needed to be in the driver's seat, to have the advantage in any sexual relationship, had wanted to stand up and cheer at that thought. Because what could be more perfect for someone who avoided intimacy than the ability to just think her way into pleasure?

"Fat lot of good it did, though," she reminded herself as she spent the morning arranging her things and settling in to the house. Because not only could she not "Thinkgasm" herself, her research had made her a laughingstock and a game-show question.

By midmorning, Lindsey realized she was starving. She'd long since exhausted her supply of cookies. They'd served as dinner last night, when she'd awakened from her long nap feeling a lot less seasick and a lot more hungry. Having no food in the house, and needing to find her way around the island before she reported to her new job in the morning, she left the cottage and headed into town.

Callie's husband, Billy, had called this morning, saying he would be home this evening and offering to show her around. Since he sounded absolutely exhausted—he'd spent every nonworking minute at the hospital—she'd refused the offer, insisting she could make it on her own. After all, Wild Boar was a tiny island, how hard could it be to navigate?

As it turned out, impossible. Not because of the size of the island, but because of the crazy rules of the road. She'd found herself about to turn onto another one-way street, and then had to detour for a washed-out bridge. By the time she reached the outskirts of Wild Boar Township, with its one stoplight, she was cranky and starving.

And then things just got better. From behind her came a blurp. A recognizable blurp.

"No way," she muttered as a flashing red-and-blue light appeared in her rearview mirror. It wasn't his big SUV, but she definitely saw a Wild Boar Island Police Department logo on the door of the car. Was Mike Santori seriously going to pull her over twice in two days? What the hell had she done this time?

Part of her was indignant. Another part, she had to admit, more than a little excited.

Despite herself, she quivered in anticipation. Her heart thudded, her breath caught in her throat. Without even being aware she was going to do it, she checked her reflection, glad she'd taken a few minutes to put on some makeup and pull her hair into a loose but pretty bun, leaving a few long strands dangling over her shoulders.

Her lightweight sweater hugged her body, the scooped neck emphasizing the top curves of her breasts. She had not dressed to impress, she swore she hadn't. But she had to admit, deep down, she'd wondered if she might run into the hunky police chief today.

She lowered her window as a tall, khaki-dressed form filled the view in her side mirror.

"This seems familiar," she said, her tone light, maybe a little flirtatious.

"You get pulled over a lot, huh?"

Lindsey immediately jerked her head and peered out the window, staring up at the cop who did not sound like Mike Santori. Didn't look like him. Wasn't him.

"Oh, no," she mumbled, seeing a young, burly guy with a bit of a paunch and carefully coiffed, slightly slick, brown hair.

"You're the new teacher, aren'tcha?"

Was it really her fate to never be called by her name again? Was everyone around here just going to call her "the new teacher" from now on?

"Yes," she said. "Is there some problem."

"How about you get out of the car?"

Oh, damn, that sounded serious. She racked her brain, trying to think of what she might have done. She could see a directional sign from here and knew she wasn't on a one-way street this time. She was pretty sure she'd used her turn signal at the last stop sign, and had definitely come to a complete stop. She certainly hadn't been speeding, not nearly comfortable enough with these narrow, windy roads to even consider it. So why on earth had he pulled her over?

"Miss?"

She reached for the door handle and opened it, stepping out. The big cop gestured her forward, pushing the door shut behind her. He then stayed there, not moving out of her way or stepping aside. He was so close his big, booted feet were only a few inches from hers. It was definitely a personal space invasion.

Her warning bells went off, as they always did around big men who used their size as an intimidation tactic. It seemed crazy to be tensing up and worrying about being alone with a uniformed cop on a sunny Sunday morning, a mile from a busy downtown area. It was broad daylight, and she was in the nicest place on the planet, according to Callie. But the truth was, she was decidedly uncomfortable, not just with this man's proximity, but with his long, assessing stare.

"What's the problem?" she asked again, crossing her arms over her chest, to which he was paying too-close attention. "I wasn't speeding, was I?"

The guy pushed his hand into the waistband of his khaki pants and scratched his gut. "Nah."

She tried to keep her annoyance in check. "Then what is it?"

"Just wanted to get a look-see."

"A...what?"

"Heard you came over on the ferry in that bright yellow tree-hugger car. Figured I'd get an eyeful of ya."

Wait. He'd pulled her over so he could see what she looked like? His expression—half interest, half cocky smirk—said he was entirely serious.

Annoyance segued to anger. "Are you telling me you pulled me over so you could check me out?"

"Yep."

The situation had gone beyond unprofessional, verging on harassment. She understood they did things differently here, but this was still the United States, and no cop, anywhere, had the right to pull someone over merely to leer at them. Even Mike, as flirtatious as he'd been yesterday, had stopped her because she was going the wrong damn way.

But this guy? What a total creep.

He proved it with his next words. "You sure are a knockout. I like that red hair."

"You had *no* right to pull me over."

"Aww, don't get hot under the collar. I was just being neighborly, wanted to welcome ya to Wild Boar."

"Next time you decide to be neighborly, tip your hat when you pass me on the street," she snapped, already turning to open her door. "And then keep on walking."

He stepped between her and the car, blocking her exit. His eyes, set deep in his fleshy face, had narrowed. She didn't imagine this bully-of-the-playground was used to anybody calling bullshit on his antics. But he quickly put that cocky smirk back on his face. "Well, cutie, there's no call for that. You might be used to people being unfriendly-like where you come from, but this here's a whole other world than what you're used to."

"No kidding. The world I come from would call this impropriety at the least, but more likely sexual harassment."

This time not only did his smile fade and his eyes narrow, an angry flush crawled up his cheeks. "Now listen here…"

"What's going on, Officer Dickinson?"

The barked question came from behind her, and Lindsey immediately swung around, relieved beyond measure to see the chief of police. Mike had pulled over across the street and approached, as quiet as a cat, his big body tense, his expression utterly serious. He cast a quick eye over her, gauging her mood, or making sure she was all right. Then he frowned at his officer. "Answer me."

"I'll tell you what's going on," Lindsey said, pushing her way past the big jerk who got turned on by red hair. "This officer pulled me over so he could 'get an eyeful' of me."

Mike's jaw tightened and his hands fisted. "Is that so?"

"Aww, calm down, no harm done. I was just saying hi."

"Complete with flashing lights and siren," she snapped.

Mike pointed an index finger at the taller man, who probably outweighed him by forty pounds. But the flab in Dickinson's brain was matched by his body, whereas Mike was all hard, powerful muscle. She had no doubt who would win in a contest of sheer, brawny strength.

"Get in your car and drive to the station," Mike said, chewing each word and then spitting it out. "I'll meet you in my office in thirty minutes."

"Oh, come on…"

"Go, Dickinson. Right now. I'm going to talk to Miss Smith and see if she wants to submit a formal complaint against you."

The big lunkhead gaped, his jaw falling down so hard it practically bounced off his chest. He stared back and forth between her and Mike, as if trying to determine whether a mark on his record was a real possibility.

It was, of course. She could file a complaint, and she probably should. She hated to admit it, but he'd made her nervous. Not afraid, necessarily, but she didn't like bullies and he'd tried to intimidate her from the minute she'd stepped out of the car. He'd covered his belligerence with small-town charm, but she'd seen right through it.

Unfortunately, getting into a fight with a local cop was not the way she wanted to start off her tenure here on the island. She didn't want to make any more of this than it already was.

Nor, however, did she want to let him off the hook right away. "Goodbye, Officer Dickinson."

The junior officer shot a fiery glare at his boss, then an equally fiery one at her, and marched, stiff-legged, to his squad car. Mike stepped closer to Lindsey, putting a hand in the small of her back, as if steadying her, and they both watched as the other vehicle tore away up the street.

"Are you all right?" Mike's voice was low, concerned, the anger still dripping from him but now equally balanced with worry.

"I'm fine. But he's an asshole."

"No kidding."

"I can't stand men who throw their weight around."

"He's got a lot of it to throw."

She grinned, as he'd probably intended her to. "Please tell me you inherited him and didn't hire him after you started?"

"Definitely inherited," Mike said. "And he's caused me nothing but grief since my first day."

"Can't you get rid of him?"

"Not only is he from a family who's lived here forever, but his uncle was the last chief. He's the one who gave good old Ollie the job."

She groaned, and not because the guy had such a stupid name. Poor Mike—talk about a rock and a hard place. It was bad enough in an office environment to have a problem employee you couldn't trust but also couldn't get rid of. As a cop, it had to be a hundred times worse. She doubted there was much violent crime here on Wild Boar, but anything could happen. Not being certain your coworkers had your back would make it much more stressful to walk into a dangerous situation.

"I'm so sorry."

"I'm the one who's sorry. This is entirely my fault— he's my responsibility. I've been trying to work with him, get him to be at least somewhat competent. Obviously we have a lot more work to do." He stared down the street in the direction the car had gone. "To be honest, he's one reason I'd like to succeed in this job. I'm afraid if I left, he'd get it by default."

"Poor Wild Boar Island."

"Exactly."

He thrust a hand through his hair, tousling the thick, brown locks. The sunlight caught glints of gold here and there in the strands and turned his dark brown eyes into something closer to amber. God, the man could be on magazine covers, yet instead here he was, standing on the side of the road, handling someone else's screwup, taking the responsibility on his own broad shoulders.

One good thing—the situation with his officer had distracted him and he hadn't mentioned what had happened yesterday at her place. She'd been half dreading running into him again, wondering how he'd behave and how she'd react. Considering all those carnal items he'd seen in her house and that kiss they'd shared, she'd feared he'd made some negative assumptions about her. Now, though, he didn't appear at all judgmental, only worried and thoughtful.

"I'd better get back to the office. Again, I'm sorry, Lindsey. I'll put the fear of God in him, but if he does anything at all, you let me know, okay?"

She nodded up at him and their stares met for a moment. He studied her face, his gaze lingering for a beat too long on her mouth. He swallowed, and she knew he'd finally allowed himself to remember yesterday.

That kiss. Oh, that kiss.

"I'll see you around," he said, his tone gruff, as if he were forcing himself to put up those barriers they'd both insisted they wanted.

"Sure."

Getting in her car, she watched in the rearview mirror as he walked back to his SUV. She would never mistake it for Dickinson's patrol car again, that was certain.

She only hoped that bastard got the message and left her alone. Though she had no doubt that if she had any problems with the other cop, Mike would take care of it. He was the caretaker type, a funny, smart, protective man wrapped up in a to-die-for sexy package.

"And you *are* going to stay away from him," she reminded herself.

But somehow, she didn't sound terribly convincing, not even to herself.

AFTER MIKE HAD his blowout with Ollie Dickinson, which ended, as usual, with the other man threatening to "tattle" to his uncle—as if the former chief would come spank Mike and make him play nice—he went home to cool off.

It took a while to get over his anger at what had happened. Lindsey was a strong woman—he knew that. Still, she shouldn't have to deal with being sexually harassed on the streets of Wild Boar. That such harassment had occurred on Mike's watch was something he would not get over anytime soon.

Although it was technically his day off, he made a point of stopping by the station house every day, just to keep things running smoothly. He should head there now, not having anything else to do. It was one o'clock on a Sunday afternoon. The church crowd would be filling the downtown eating establishments for their Sunday brunches. A whole townful of people would probably welcome him to join them at their tables, or in their homes, or at the station, or the shops.

But none of those options appealed. The only place that really appealed to him right now was a small cottage on the southern tip of the island. In that cottage lived the only other person who probably understood how he felt—like a fish out of water. He'd bet she was also spending a quiet Sunday alone, maybe reading a book.

Yeah, but what kind of book?

He pushed that thought away, not allowing himself to remember those wild moments he and Lindsey had shared yesterday. He'd spent enough time dreaming about them last night.

But maybe he should stop by and make sure she'd gotten something to eat. Plus, he was worried about the heat in the old place. And he also wanted to ensure she had a working phone, since she was so far from any neighbors and cell service on the island was notoriously spotty.

Hell, he wanted to take care of her. That probably wouldn't surprise anybody who knew him well—Mike had always been the overprotective one in his family. Lindsey wouldn't appreciate it, though. He'd already figured out she liked her independence, liked being in control at all times.

Interesting then, that she'd chosen teaching as a profession. He'd always associated teachers with traits such as being nurturing, patient and generous. Lindsey certainly had those qualities, but they were definitely outweighed by her determination, frankness, wit and sex appeal. It was an interesting combination.

Interesting? Hell. Try fascinating.

He'd begun to wonder if she might be exactly the type of woman he'd been looking for. Smart enough to keep up with him, but with a nice, normal job, not one that made her so ruthlessly ambitious she'd dump a guy still recovering from a slit throat.

Even putting Lindsey in the same thought as his ex seemed wrong, and he quickly shoved the whole subject out of his mind. He wasn't going to see her without a good reason or an invitation. Period.

Instead, to cut through the silence, he got online and pulled up Skype. His parents had gotten their first computer recently and had become addicted to video chatting. Waiting for the connection, he forced a smile onto his face, knowing his intuitive mother would see something was wrong even with the expression.

"Little brother!"

It wasn't his mother. Leo had responded, apparently at the folks' house for a typical Sunday get-together. Since Leo and Madison had gotten married a few weeks ago, the two of them were really settling into the whole family routine. That was probably in preparation for the birth of their own little girl, due in three months.

His brother was going to be a father. It was hard to believe. Leo, a firefighter, had had a near miss with a real piranha of a woman that he'd been engaged to a while back. At first, Mike and their oldest brother, Rafe, had been worried Leo's thing with Madison Reid might have been a rebound romance. They had met, after all, when Leo had gone for his prepaid honeymoon to Costa Rica. Alone.

The fact that Madison was the former fiancée of a Hollywood superstar had made them that much more nervous. At least until they'd met her. Seeing the love between the two had set everyone's mind at ease.

Then, of course, Rafe had come home for Christmas with a woman they all remembered he'd dated years ago, but had believed was out of his life for good. Uh-uh. Rafe and Ellie were engaged, planning to wed when Rafe rotated stateside later this year.

His brothers were settling down as rapidly as his cousins had a few years ago, tipping over, one after another, like pins in a bowling alley.

"How's it goin'?" he asked Leo through the screen, already knowing the answer to that question.

"Fantastic. Wanna see a picture of the baby?"

"Isn't she still cooking?"

"Yeah, but these sonograms, you just can't believe the detail!"

Mike's instant message notifier dinged. He clicked over and opened the fuzzy image his brother had just sent him, with the vague shape of a kidney bean in the middle. Leaning closer, he was able to distinguish head from feet, but not much more than that.

"Nice," he murmured, looking into the camera again.

"I know, right? So how's life treating you?"

He shrugged. "Same."

"Ready to bail and come home yet?"

"I'm not a quitter."

"Never believed you were. I meant, have you booked your trip home the day after your six months are up?"

Laughing, Mike shook his head. "Don't think so. I intend to make this work. Chicago P.D.'s not an option anymore."

Leo nodded, his good humor fading as he frowned in concern. "Are you okay? Everything healed up?"

Mike rubbed his fingers against the scar on his neck. It was still red, but the tenderness had faded…physically, at least. Emotionally, he wasn't sure it ever would. "Yeah. I'm fine. I guess I just haven't quite figured out what I wanna do when I grow up."

"Well, there are a couple of people who might have some options for you to consider."

His interest piqued, Mike raised a curious brow. "Who?"

"The twins."

"Mark and Nick?" His cousins were a little older, so growing up, he, Leo and Rafe had looked up to all five of the boys on that branch of the Santori family tree.

"Yeah. They called Mama the other day and got your contact info. Sounds like they want to talk to you about some kind of business idea."

Hmm. Interesting.

Mark was a cop, so Mike had crossed paths with him a lot at work, though they'd been at different precincts. Nick was in security, having gotten out of the Marines and become a bouncer at a strip club where his wife, Izzie, had headlined. Weird. But they made it work.

"I'm open to hearing their idea," he admitted.

"We'd love to have you back in Chi-town, man. It's gonna suck doing the daddy thing without Uncle Mikey around to lend a hand. Who's gonna scare off all the boys who start coming around when my baby girl hits puberty?"

"I think you're more than capable of that," he said with a dry chuckle.

"I'm a lover, not a fighter. Madison says I'm going to be the first human-shape marshmallow when the kid gets big enough to start wrapping me around her little finger."

Probably true. With his huge heart, Leo was the nicest of the brothers, so generous and easygoing. Rafe…well, he was a bit of a hard-ass and sure didn't have Leo's breezy outlook on life. After so many years in Afghanistan, that was probably understandable. Ellie, however, seemed to have softened him some.

Then there was him, Mike. The youngest, the cop, the one who had never seen an abused animal he didn't want to take in, or met a bully he hadn't ended up punching out.

That was probably why he'd joined the force to begin with.

It was also probably why he'd left.

There was only so much head-banging-against-the-wall he could reasonably do. He'd never been able to *really* make a difference, and nearly losing his life while failing at his job just didn't mesh with his genetic code.

He and Leo BS'd a little while longer, then his parents came into the room and waved from the background. His mom raised her voice to shouting level, as if she feared she wasn't being picked up by the microphone, and Mike pushed his seat away from the speakers just to get a little relief.

Damn, how he missed his family. All of them. Parents, siblings, cousins, aunts and uncles. He had thought when he'd left Chicago that going to a place where there were no other Santoris would be good for him, a welcome change. He'd wanted to figure things out in a place where he had to stand completely on his own and would be by himself to think.

He just hadn't realized that he wasn't cut out to be a loner until recently.

For some reason, that brought Lindsey to his mind. He wondered if she had figured that out about herself yet. And if she had possibly considered the fact that maybe the two of them, as the outsiders, the loners, might in fact be a perfect match. If only it weren't for their jobs.

5

ALTHOUGH LINDSEY HAD never taught kids, she'd put in plenty of days as a teacher's assistant throughout her academic career. That meant subbing for professors a lot of the time. Before starting this new job, she'd figured teaching college freshmen wouldn't be that much different than teaching high school seniors. And really, it wasn't.

These kindergartners, though? Oh, man. They were going to be the death of her.

"Miss Smiff, Maffew took all the gween cwayons so nobody else can color their twees."

Blinking as she interpreted that rare dialect known as six-years-old-and-toothless, Lindsey sighed and swiped her hand through her hair. It was only first period, and she was a teacher, so a margarita was out of the question. But oh, could she use one.

After being on the job for only five days, she had already decided Callie should be canonized. Lindsey had no idea how her friend—or any of the teachers at the Wild Boar School—did it.

First off, she taught six classes a day and only had one brief planning period that wasn't long enough to catch her breath, much less grade papers or prepare lessons. During the first period, this one, she taught all the K–3 kids. In the classroom, the kids were separated by grade into smaller work groups, and she spent the entire class period revolving between them, giving mini lectures to one while praying the others would stay on task with what she'd asked them to work on.

The kindergartners rarely did. And her classroom "assistant"—one of the moms—spent more time helping her own kid with his classwork than she did keeping things running smoothly when Lindsey's back was turned.

After this period, she would move on to the fourth through sixth graders. Same setup. Then seventh and eighth. Ditto.

This afternoon, she'd get ninth grade biology, then tenth grade chemistry. Finally, at the very end of the day, advanced chemistry, which had eight students, all seniors, all vying to be valedictorian of their seventy-five-person graduating class.

Frankly, she'd rather have all seventy-five of those seniors in her physics class than try to have four eyes in her head to keep track of grades K-1-2-3.

"Miss Smiff, did you heaw me? Maffew's not being vewy nice. Do *you* think it's nice to keep all the gween cwayons?"

"No, it's not very nice," she admitted, turning away from the third graders. Again.

From the beginning, her strategy had been to connect all of her class lessons so that each group's subject was somehow related to the others. Today, she'd been talking to the kids about plant life. Nothing along the lines of oxygenation and photosynthesis…strictly, why some trees have flowers and others don't. But the blank expressions on the faces of the kindergartners this morning, and their fidgeting bodies, had made her give that up and go right to the old I'm-not-a-parent-and-have-no-idea-how-to-handle-little-kids standby: coloring. Specifically, coloring sheets printed with bushes, trees and flowers, most of which required green. It appeared Maffew hadn't remembered that whole "sharing" thing.

"I'll talk to him, Sarah."

"I'm Emily."

Oh. Right. She had only been on the job five days and hadn't memorized all the kids' names. That would have been impossible in so short a time, of course. But considering in this room alone there were four Sarahs and five Emilys, one of those two was usually a good bet if she was at a loss. For the boys? Jason and Michael.

Mike.

Even during the day, there was one Mike who just wouldn't get out of her head... The one who'd seen her sex-toy collection and then kissed her like he wanted to use every item in it with her. The encounter they'd shared—that embrace, that kiss—wouldn't leave her mind. Nor would the memory of the expression on his face as he'd wondered what she did with those toys when she was alone.

She hadn't been kidding when she'd told him she wasn't in the market for romance or relationships. But that didn't mean she couldn't imagine having fabulous sex with him.

It had gotten so bad that at night she'd been tempted to actually use one of those vibrators, to take the pressure off. She might have written about the Thinkgasm, might have interviewed women who could think themselves off, but she hadn't mastered the art herself. Lying in bed fantasizing about that strong body of his, that great laugh, the amazing mouth and that hot, wonderful kiss, only made her more frustrated, and certainly didn't do anything to relieve the tension.

She hadn't ended up trying any of the toys, though.

Despite what he'd assumed, she'd never used any of the things from that box.

She'd seen Mike around town this week, and had always stopped to say hello. He was usually putting out fires that seemed terribly important to the locals…like taking a report on somebody's stolen trash can or coming to the school to do an anti-drinking talk with the older students. They hadn't, however, been alone together since that unpleasant scene with his coworker Sunday morning.

She missed him. Crazy, since they'd only known each other a week, but it was true. Whenever she spotted him, her heart thumped and her pulse roared. She wanted nothing more than to find some excuse to be alone with him, even while her sensible side screamed at her not to be an idiot.

"Miss Smiff? Are you coming?"

Hearing the six-year-old's impatience, she shook off the crazy thoughts and focused on her job. "Yes, I'm coming, Emily."

Giving quick instructions to the third graders, she turned back to the little ones, sorted out the crayon catastrophe, and then moved through the rest of the class.

The remainder of the day was much the same. Just as she had on the previous four days, she found herself enjoying the older kids in her seventh period class. If she had an entire day of high school honors kids, she might actually choose to stick with this teaching gig for a while. It sure beat being ridiculed or made the butt of sexy jokes by the media. But the herding-cats feel of the younger groups was going to drive her nuts.

Fortunately, she'd become friendly with several of the other teachers, all of whom had been welcoming. They'd offered advice on everything from dealing with classroom misbehavior, to life on the island. Not at all to her surprise, two of them warned her about Officer Ollie Dickinson, who had a thing for pulling over single women.

At the end of the day, one of those teachers popped her head in. "You've survived another day!"

She smiled, remembering the pretty young woman's name was Teresa and she taught elementary-age English. She and a few of the other teachers had taken Lindsey under their wing. "Five down."

"Any hot plans for the weekend?"

"Did I miss a happening downtown club scene here?"

Teresa smirked. "Yeah, uh…no. You'll have to take the ferry to the mainland for that."

"Not a chance. I haven't recovered from my trip over." Even if it had allowed her to meet the amazingly sexy chief.

"Okay, well, have a great weekend!"

"Thanks," she said, appreciating the brief check-in. It had been a nice thing to do.

For the most part, everybody on Wild Boar was just as friendly. Her landlady had made a point of stopping by with more cookies, the cashiers at the shops were always cheerful, the waitresses at the diner always laughed and chatted. It was all so very…nice.

She wished she could say she loved that, but she was too much of a big-city girl not to find it all just a little suspicious. Too much niceness made her teeth ache, and she really wished Callie were around to add a wee bit of snark to her day.

After school, wanting an injection of caffeine, she went to her favorite new haunt. The main street of the town, which bore the same name as the island, was about a mile long, and was lined mostly with walk-ups and small businesses. Mom-and-pop shops, a drugstore, a bakery, a hobby shop and a couple of restaurants operated year-round. She'd noticed signs on some of the craft and antiques businesses that said they would reopen in May, in time for tourist season.

The coffee shop, though, called The Daily Grind, was open all day, every day, and that's where she headed. She pushed the door in, bringing a strong spring breeze with her, and the heads of everyone inside turned to watch her enter. From behind the counter, the owner, a happy-looking, middle-aged woman named Angie, smiled and called out a greeting. Nicely, of course. "Hi, Lindsey. Extra-large coffee with two creams and two sugars?"

She'd never lived in a place where the people not only knew their customers by their first names, but also remembered how they took their coffee. In Chicago, Lindsey had stopped at the same chain café near her apartment a couple of times a week for two years and had seldom seen the same barista twice.

"Sounds great."

Angie got to work as Lindsey headed over. "How's everything going over at the school?"

"Just fine."

"What about Callie and the baby? Have you talked to her lately. Is he doing well?"

Nodding, Lindsey replied, "It sounds like baby William is doing much better. Callie has called me several times to give me lots of tips and advice about handling 'her' kids."

"You tell her for me to stop worrying about anybody else's little ones and just focus on her own precious angel."

"I will," Lindsey said, glad to hear the warmth and fondness in the older woman's voice.

Whether Lindsey was comfortable with it or not, the niceness definitely benefited Callie. She hadn't lived here long—two years, maybe—but the town had claimed Callie as one of their own after her marriage to Billy, a local boy. Everybody was concerned about her and the baby.

Lindsey hadn't seen Billy since her arrival. He was either working or at the hospital, wanting to be there for his wife during these early, touch-and-go stages of their son's life. But everywhere she went, people sang his praises, too, which made her feel more confident about her dearest friend's life here.

"Here you go," Angie said, pushing a white ceramic mug toward her. "T.G.I.C."

"Huh?"

"Thank God It's Caffeinated."

She grinned, liking the woman, and replied, "You've got that right."

Taking her coffee, she headed to an empty café table in the back. The shop had free wireless internet access, one of the few places on Wild Boar that did. Since she hadn't had time to get anybody to come out to the cottage to wire her up, and the school's wireless blocked a lot of sites to keep the kids off social media during the school day, she had to do her emailing and catching up on Facebook from here.

Opening her laptop, she booted it up, sipped the hot coffee and glanced around the shop. She recognized a few faces. There were two other teachers, at whom she smiled. A couple of strangers offered her cautious but friendly nods, obviously knowing who she was. A trio of her honors students sprawled in a circle of lounge chairs in the front window, chatting and using their laptops. They waved at her with enthusiasm.

"We're doing our homework," one of them, a pretty blond-haired girl, called from across the room.

"Sure you are," she replied with a wry lift of a brow. "Just don't rely on Twitter to help with next week's exam."

The kids laughed good-naturedly, going back to their conversation, and Lindsey began to flip through her email. She immediately deleted the dozen interview requests that had come in since yesterday. Also deleted were the obligatory penis-enlarging, Russian bride and overseas finance minister scams.

That left her with two emails, one of which was from Callie. Attached to it was a picture of the baby, so tiny in his incubator. At least she could see him now, unlike when she'd gone to visit at the hospital ten days ago. His precious face had been covered with a mask, his body frail and weak-looking. He appeared much stronger now, bigger, too, and judging by the tone of her friend's email, was growing beautifully. That made Lindsey's whole Wild Boar ordeal worthwhile, in her opinion.

Surfing onto Facebook, she checked her private page, accessible only to real friends. She'd deleted her professional one when the comments had gotten absolutely unbearable.

Once she'd finished her online stuff, she slowly sipped her coffee, somehow loath to leave this little slice of society and return to her quiet, empty house. After living in Chicago for several years, she just wasn't used to silence. She had never felt more alone than she had since this move, not having had one visitor since Mike left on Saturday.

By four, she realized she couldn't take up a table while continuing to nurse one cup of coffee, so she began to pack up her stuff to leave. She unzipped her laptop case and slid her computer into it, paying no attention to the ringing of the bell over the coffee shop door.

At least, not at first.

Then she heard Angie greet the newcomer. And she could do nothing else *but* pay attention as the dark-haired, dark-eyed man in khaki walked in and headed to the counter.

"Howya doin', Chief?" asked Angie.

It was the very person she'd been unable to stop thinking about. The very one she'd had those wild and wicked dreams about.

The very one she needed to avoid.

"Good, thanks." Mike Santori offered the woman a slight smile and a nod, looking around and giving the same casual greeting to everyone else.

Until his eyes landed on Lindsey. With her he didn't smile, nod and move on. Instead, his eyes widened and his mouth parted on a quick inhalation that she could almost hear.

Her heart thudded and her stomach churned. She realized her hand was shaking when her nearly empty coffee mug rattled enough to splash a small amount of lukewarm coffee against her fingers. Lowering it, she forced herself to take a steadying breath. She was going to be here for weeks; she needed to get used to running into him. She simply couldn't afford to be embarrassed about what had happened between them on Saturday.

It's not embarrassment.

She tried to hush the voice in her head, even as she acknowledged it was right. Yes, there was some embarrassment about the things he'd witnessed, and the fact that she'd fallen into his arms so soon after they'd met. But mostly what she felt when she saw Mike Santori was this strange, urgent tension. Currently her blood was gushing and a sort of electric energy surged through her, making the hairs on her arms stand up. Her foot was tapping on the floor, her fingers doing the same on the table, as if she just needed to move.

It was awareness. Attraction, too. She hadn't been able to get Mike out of her mind since the moment they'd met.

"Here you go, Chief," Angie said, handing him a foam cup with a lid. Obviously he was taking his to go.

Lindsey held her breath, wondering if he would leave

without a word to her. After everything they'd said on Saturday, about how neither of them was interested in any romantic entanglements, what they should do was continue exchanging nothing more than those polite smiles in public. If he actually sat with her and started a conversation, the gossipers would have them engaged by midnight.

She knew that, knew she should be hoping he'd turn around and leave. But instead, something inside her blossomed and warmed at the idea of him sitting in the empty seat at her table. And within fifteen seconds, he was.

"Is this seat taken?"

"You've just taken it," she pointed out, trying, unsuccessfully, to hide a smile at that fact.

"True." He sipped his coffee, eyeing her over the cup. "How are you doing, Lindsey?"

"Fine, thanks. No more seasickness."

"The island doesn't move quite as much as the ferry did." There was a twinkle in those brown eyes, and little crinkles beside them. The guy whose very career should make him dour, was quick-to-smile, instead. She liked that about him. Among the many things she liked about him.

His mouth, his hands, his body.

His kiss. Oh, good lord did the man know how to kiss!

She shook off the thoughts and replied, "That's good. I doubt I'd survive another sea voyage anytime soon."

"Are you settling into the cottage okay?"

"It's a little drafty," she admitted. "Being close to the lake, those watery winds tend to sift through the eaves. But I've got lots of blankets on my bed."

Shit, Lindsey. Don't talk about your bed with this man. Because, if you do, the look on your face will make it clear to everyone in the room that you wouldn't mind if he shared that bed.

Fortunately, Mike didn't take the opening she'd so stu-

pidly left there. Probably because, unlike Saturday, they
were surrounded by curious busybodies.

He leaned over the table, keeping his voice low. "Have
you had any more problems with…anybody?"

"Not a one," she said, knowing he was referring to his
obnoxious junior officer.

"Good. I've been trying to keep him busy."

"I appreciate it."

He nodded and asked, "What about the job? How's
school?"

"It's okay," she said, lifting her own cup. "Different."

"You know, you mentioned that you're not regularly a
teacher, but you never did tell me what your real job is."

He waited. She didn't respond, trying to figure out how
to answer the unasked question.

Finally, he said, "Okay, state secret."

"No, it's not," she said, feeling stupid. *But yes, it is.*
"I'm sort of unemployed right now. That's why this substitute position worked out so well, for me and for Callie."

"Where did you work before?"

"In Chicago." She'd intentionally misinterpreted the
question, sticking to geography.

That appeared to surprise him. Obviously he hadn't
read her license very closely last week when he'd pulled
her over. "Really? Me, too."

"Oh!" He'd mentioned he was a recent transplant. Dumb
of her to never ask where he'd come from. "Where did
you live?"

"Little Italy. Near the university. I worked for the Chicago P.D."

Now she was one who was surprised. "Seriously?"

"Yeah. I started when I was twenty as a beat cop. Kept
going to college at night, worked my way up. After I finished school, I landed my detective shield."

"You were a Chicago Police detective, and now you're..."

"Chief of the Tinytown Police Department?" He sighed, sounding rueful. "Yep. And, before you ask, it was my choice. I didn't get fired for taking bribes or anything of that sort."

"That thought *never* crossed my mind." She might not know him well—yet—but she was already sure Mike Santori was one of the good guys. "Are you happy with your decision?"

"I guess. It hasn't all been chocolate-chip cookies and helping old ladies cross the street, you know."

"I'll bet."

"There are some really big pluses to living here rather than in Chicago, especially in my line of work."

"Such as?"

"Not getting shot at."

She winced, hating the idea of it. His tone might be light, but his expression was very serious. He *had* been shot at. Given the crime statistics of her home city, that wasn't surprising. She even knew a few civilians who'd been shot at and couldn't imagine what it would be like to be a cop in such a dangerous city. She sent up a mental prayer of thanks that he'd gotten out, and not just because she was glad to have met him.

"That's always a bonus," she replied, keeping things light, not asking the questions she was dying to ask—namely, who, what, when, where and why. "Is there anything else you enjoy?"

"Well, although I miss them, I do sort of enjoy being fairly sure I'm not going to run into some member of my family every damn time I leave my house."

She couldn't contain a small laugh. "Only fairly sure?"

"A posse of them will show up here one of these days.

I'm the first Santori to move further than fifty miles away from Chicago."

"So you have a big family?"

"Enormous."

She considered that, wondering what it would be like. Being an only child of pretty screwed-up parents, who'd seldom worried about feeding or clothing the one kid they had, she suspected it was a good thing she didn't have any siblings. Callie was like a sister to her, and Callie's family, though almost as poor as her own, had provided her with a lot of the love and warmth she'd missed out on at home.

The lack of money made some people desperate and cold, while it made others far more appreciative of the things—and people—they did have. Thankfully, Callie's folks had been the grateful sort, with hearts big enough to welcome a kid whose parents were not.

Suddenly thinking about Mike's last name, and remembering a restaurant she'd gone to a couple of times in the city, she asked, "Are you related to the Santoris who own a pizza joint on Taylor Avenue?"

He nodded. "My Uncle Tony and Aunt Rosa founded it. My cousin Tony runs it now, with his wife, Gloria."

"Great food."

"I know." He shook his head mournfully. "I haven't had a decent slice of pizza since I moved here. The only Italian place on the island is run by a family named Fitzpatrick."

"Irish-Italian. That's a good combination, so I hear." She immediately told herself to forget the fact that she was about seventy-five percent Irish and he looked about as Italian as the Godfather's Godfather.

"They have corned-beef-and-cabbage calzone on the menu."

She snorted. Realizing he wasn't even smiling—and

was, in fact, serious, she thought about it and mused, "Actually, that sounds pretty fantastic."

"That's it. You're banned from Italy for life."

"Dang. And it's on my bucket list, too."

"Maybe you just need to learn how to appreciate real Italian food," he told her, his brown eyes warming. "I'm a great cook."

Her heart fluttered. To busy her hands, she reached for her cup and toyed with the handle, scraping the tip of her finger across the smooth edge. "Really?"

"My mom regretted not having a daughter to pass her secret recipes on to, so she taught me and both my brothers a few of her specialties."

Brothers. Plural. More Mikes in the world? Good grief.

"I could…"

"Chief, there you are!"

Lindsey jerked her attention to the barrel-chested man who suddenly appeared beside their small table. She couldn't help wondering just what Mike had been about to say before they were interrupted. *I could…cook for you? Teach you? Give you ten kinds of orgasm in twenty minutes?*

She'd never know. And that was just as well. Because as she glanced around the shop, she noticed they were being stared at by everyone in it. She'd prefer to believe it had been the loud proclamation of the man who'd interrupted them that had called the patrons' attention, but she seriously doubted it. If she could go back in time thirty seconds, she'd bet she would still see those same wide-eyed, titillated faces watching their table.

"I have to talk to you about that no-parking zone out in front of my shop."

Probably about sixty, the stranger had iron-gray hair, cut military close, and a broad face, half-hidden behind a bushy beard. Why he'd chosen to cut the hair off his head only to grow it on his face, she had no idea, but the result was a little jarring.

Mike rose to his feet with a heavy sigh, as if he'd had this conversation before. "Mr. Winpigler, you *know* I can't change the zoning and let you park vehicles out front, not when there's a fire hydrant practically right outside your door."

"That hydrant is in a very inconvenient location!"

"I'll bet you wouldn't say that if your shop caught fire."

Lindsey put her hand over her mouth to hide a chuckle. Mike certainly had the other man there.

"I still want to talk about it. That is, if you can tear yourself away." The man spared a quick look at Lindsey, a look she didn't like. It was assessing, a little dismissive, as if she were some bimbo distracting the chief from his oh-so-important job settling parking space disputes.

She got up, grabbing her purse and her laptop case. "I should go."

Mike glanced at her, and then around the room. Finally noticing they were the center of attention—and not just because the local business owner had a loud mouth— he didn't try to talk her into staying. "Nice running into you," he said with an impersonal nod, as if they barely knew each other.

Nice try. She doubted it would help. A ten-minute conversation had landed them on the local radar; people would be talking about their coffee-shop interlude all weekend.

It was ridiculous to think something so innocent could bring about any kind of scandal. But this was a small town. She'd spent part of her childhood in one, and was familiar with how things worked. No, she wasn't the daughter of a drunk and a drug addict here in Wild Boar, but she *was* an outsider. And considering she was the new teacher—

the protector of all the innocent minds of their precious children—and Mike was the chief of police—responsible for their safety—of course she and Mike were going to be living under everyone's watchful eye.

The last thing she needed right now was to draw any more attention to herself; she'd had quite enough of that in recent months. Nor did she want to reflect badly on Callie, who would have to live amongst these people long after Lindsey was gone, back in her real life and her real career.

There was also Mike's new job to consider. He had to be on shaky ground this early in his employment. Considering he'd left Chicago to save his very *life*, how could she possibly do anything that would put his new job at risk?

That wasn't all. This place wasn't cut off from the rest of the world—she'd just spent an hour on the internet, for heaven's sake! If people started talking about her and Mike, might somebody not decide they wanted to learn a little more about the new schoolteacher? Luckily Lindsey Smith was a very common name, and it wouldn't be that easy to find her. Still, somebody who was really determined certainly could, and they'd find a lot of snarky humor and nasty innuendo that she just couldn't deal with right now. Next she'd get the same treatment from the people on the island—she'd no longer be Callie's nice friend who was pitching in at the school, she'd be a sex fiend who might warp the minds of their precious little angels.

So yeah, it was time to get out of the café, far away from Mike Santori and his dark, dreamy eyes and soft, sexy mouth. She needed to escape his temptation, the kind that was making her forget she was here to lie low and escape being talked about because of sex and orgasms... even if all she could think about when he was around was having sex and orgasms.

Nodding at Mike and his irate citizen, she hurried

past them, mumbling, "Thanks for the information, Chief Santori."

Right—loads of information. She now knew not to shop at Mr. Loudmouth's store, and what kind of calzone to order from the local pizzeria. The most important bit of information she'd gotten from Mike, however, was that he was one hell of a great guy.

"Bye, Lindsey!" the woman behind the counter called.

The goodbye was echoed by Lindsey's students, who, unlike the adults in the place, appeared more interested in their online activities than in her personal ones, thank goodness.

Hurrying outside, she immediately turned toward the municipal parking lot, which was located behind the public school. She'd discovered, just as Mike had warned, that the parking situation at the school was terrible. Not because there were that many cars, but there were simply too few spaces. So she'd taken to leaving her Prius in the town lot. When tourist season started, that might be a problem, but for now, her cute yellow car sat entirely alone in the lot, looking like a sunny-side-up egg in the middle of a cast-iron skillet.

Reaching the driver's side, she searched for her keys. She remembered she'd dropped them into her laptop bag instead of her purse this morning, and flipped it open. As she dug around in the side pocket, she realized someone was calling her name.

"Lindsey, wait up!"

She glanced over the hood of her car, seeing Mike walking toward her across the parking lot. Damn. So much for a clean getaway. What was he thinking, following her like this? He had to have noticed how much attention they'd been drawing inside.

"What can I do for you, Chief?"

"We didn't finish our conversation."

"Yes, we did."

"I was about to offer you a home-cooked meal."

"And I was about to decline," she insisted, still digging for the elusive keys. In fact, she dug so forcefully, the shoulder strap of her laptop case slipped, and she dropped the whole thing onto the ground.

"Damn it," she said, nervous and irritated, wondering why the man flustered her so. She just prayed the bag's padding had prevented any damage to the equipment inside.

"Calm down," he ordered, reaching her car as she bent to grab her bag. "We're not being watched by the secret police."

She scanned the area, frowning. "We are, however, being watched by the kids over there on the basketball court, the old man walking his dog across the street and the woman pushing the baby stroller at the intersection."

He turned his head to look, obviously realizing she was not exaggerating. Even from several feet away, she noted that his jaw flexed as he clenched it. His broad shoulders also stiffened, his body radiating frustration.

"We've both already realized that if we talk to each other we're going to draw attention, and neither of us wants that," she said. "So I should just get out of here."

"Christ," he muttered. "Why can't people mind their own business? This is worse than my family."

"We're both newcomers, and we're both in positions that the public feels they have a right to comment on," she said, blowing out her own frustrated breath. "You don't want them to say that their new chief is distracted by a pretty face."

That had come out wrong, made her sound cocky, and she hadn't intentionally been trying to pay herself a compliment. But he was smart enough to figure out what she'd been trying to say. "I also don't want them to believe their kids' new teacher is a… What did you call me? A sex addict?"

He winced. "I apologized for that, didn't I?"

"Yes. At any rate, I need to go home, and you need to stay here. Plus, we both agreed we weren't looking for any romantic entanglements."

"I'm not talking about *tangling* you."

A twinkle in his eye said he'd considered saying something else. Maybe something about doing more than tangling, like, say, tying. Or handcuffing.

Good lord, she'd never in a million years thought *that* fantasy would appeal to her. Something about Mike, though, knowing how strong yet protective he was, how decent, made her wonder about it. Made her, in fact, a little melty-limbed.

She stiffened those limbs, and her resolve. "We both said…"

"I remember what I said. But maybe I'm getting a little tired of worrying about what other people will think. I shouldn't have to check over my shoulder every time I have a conversation."

"I can certainly understand that," she said. She'd only been here a week and she already felt stifled. She couldn't imagine how bad it was for him.

"If I'm going to make a life here, I need to start living it on my terms."

A life here. He'd seemed to be on the fence before, but now he sounded like he really intended to stay on Wild Boar. For someone like Mike—with a huge family, born and bred in Chicago—it was a pretty dramatic decision. His old job must have really been dangerous for this to be the future he chose.

"So what do you say?"

"What changed from last week when you weren't interested?"

"Oh, honey, I was interested the moment I set eyes on you on that ferry," he assured her, the warmth in his voice matching the warmth in his eyes.

She crossed her arms and hugged herself, determined not to let that admission lower her guard.

"The truth is, I've been thinking about the kind of woman I might be looking for. Not just for sex, but for more than that, and every minute I've spent with you has made me want you that much more."

He wasn't just talking about a fling? He wanted to pursue something more serious with her? The realization left her reeling.

"I always seemed to end up with the wrong type in Chicago, but maybe the right type might be right in front of my face."

"What type might that be?" she asked, interested despite herself. What was Mike really looking for?

"Somebody trustworthy."

Check.

"Somebody smart, adventurous. Nice."

Yep. Yep. Sometimes.

So far, so good.

"Somebody who wants the simple things and isn't so busy climbing a corporate ladder she can't spare a minute of compassion for anybody else."

That sounded like a story. Before she could ask him about it, though, he continued.

"A small-town teacher who's gorgeous and funny as hell seems to fit the bill."

Small-town teacher? Simple? Not a ladder-climber?

Oy. Those definitely didn't describe her. It might sound

like the Lindsey he was getting to know, but he didn't know the real woman.

Sadness stabbed her, because, the truth was, if he did meet the real her, he probably wouldn't be interested anymore.

"So?" He stepped closer. "Give me a chance. Give us a chance."

She let out a heavy sigh.

She wasn't the kind of woman he wanted. She was too susceptible to his charm, already too eager to spend time with him. But if he asked her to come over so he could cook her dinner, she'd probably stay through breakfast, and they both knew it.

She did not want to be the kindergarten teacher who did the walk of shame a week after her arrival in the nicest town on earth. Especially because, after the sex, she greatly feared she'd still be left with the liking, the admiration, all the damned *emotions* she didn't want to have about any man she slept with.

And when he found out who she really was, what she really did and why she was here, he probably wouldn't have any feelings toward her at all. Other than resentment or anger if she ended up costing him a job he needed and wanted.

No. It couldn't happen. They couldn't work.

"I'm sorry, Mike," she said, pleading with her eyes for him not to press her. "I just can't."

He stared at her in silence, watching her face, as if to gauge her determination. She sensed he was disappointed in her, even though she'd been honest from the beginning about what she was here for…and what she was *not here for*. He might have had the kind of week that made him change his mind. She hadn't.

"All right," he said with a resigned shrug. "You win."

No, actually, she hadn't won. In fact, she greatly feared they had both lost something. But considering where she was at this point in her life, there was really nothing she could do about it. Which just might break her heart, even if she *didn't* have the guts to open it up and let a smart, sexy guy into it.

6

"CHIEF, WE HAVE a problem, a very serious problem. I demand that you do something about it."

Mike glanced up from the paperwork he'd been filling out—a requisition for some new computer equipment for use by the dispatcher—as his previously closed office door burst open without a warning knock. A member of the island's governing council stormed in, bringing a cloud of righteous indignation and heavy perfume with her.

"Hello, Mrs. Franklin. Have a seat."

He wondered if she heard the surprise in his voice. She was a pain in the ass, but she usually only barged in during daylight hours. It was now midevening, close to 9:00 p.m., and he'd expected a quiet Saturday night until his shift ended at ten. But apparently it wasn't to be

He closed his folder, clicked his pen and put it down, watching as the tall, stick-thin woman with the blue-gray hair situated herself on the edge of the chair fronting his desk. She was probably his least favorite member of the council, being one of the stuffiest, most uptight people he'd met since moving here.

Mrs. Franklin was a descendent of one of the town founders and never let anyone forget it. She ran a general store up the street and considered herself the premiere businessperson of Wild Boar, having an opinion about everything and everyone. The other council members were men, and every one of them was terrified of her. He'd only been here a few months, but he was beginning to understand why. The woman had the constitution of a pit bull hidden in that gaunt frame.

"Now, what seems to be the problem?" he asked, tenting his fingers on his desk.

"Someone is peddling smut in Wild Boar," she snapped.

His finger-tent fell. "Excuse me?"

"Filth is filling our streets, damaging the brains of our youth and threatening our entire way of life. Mainland corruption and vice have spilled into the water and landed on our shores."

Wow. Quite a speech. And judging by the precisely chosen words and deliberate emphasis, a speech she'd rehearsed before coming in here. The violent nodding of her head and twitching of her mouth said she was working herself up to continue.

He cut her off before she could. "Why don't you tell me what the problem is."

"The problem is the insidious intrusion of pornography into our community."

"Pornography?"

She jerked her chin up, her mouth tightening to the size of a quarter in disgust as she reached into her large purse and pulled out a towel-wrapped object. She dropped it onto his desk with a deep, pained grimace.

"See for yourself."

He was almost scared to look. What, he wondered, would this prude of a woman constitute as pornography? Had somebody lent her the DVD set of the second season of *Friends* or something?

His curiosity aroused, he unfolded the corners of the towel, realizing right away the item was too small to be a DVD case. In fact, it was only about three-by-five inches, and was actually a book.

Reading the title, he held back a smile. Though the color illustration on the front was graphic, it was also artistic. As, he'd heard, was this particular book.

"Do you see?" she asked, tapping the tip of her finger on his desk with a sharp little peck. "Filth."

"Ma'am, this is a copy of the *Kama Sutra*." *Not* Big Tits and Dongs on Parade.

"I can read, Chief Santori," the woman said, her tone as tart as her personality.

"I don't think this book is considered pornography. In fact, it's a revered, ancient Indian text, I believe."

"Smut," she said, leaning forward and whipping the book open. She swiped her fingers through the pages, angrily tapping at the illustrations. "Just look!"

"Umm. Interesting," he said, trying to figure out how *that* could go *there*. "Where did you get this?"

"It was discovered on the very streets of our town." She fanned herself with her hand. If she'd had some smelling salts on hand, he'd bet she'd use them to fortify herself for this horrible mission she'd undertaken. "A child found it. Can you imagine? A vulnerable child."

Oh, hell. That was pretty awkward. "Who was it?"

"Annie Morgan's son, Tim."

Mike frowned. If he was remembering correctly, the Morgan boy was a senior in high school. Not exactly an innocent first grader emotionally damaged by glimpsing some artistically drawn sexual positions.

"Annie discovered it in his room."

Huh. Tim Morgan should find better places to hide the stuff he didn't want mommy to see. Hell, Mike and his brother Leo, who'd shared a room growing up, had pulled the grating out of their heater element to stash their *Playboy* magazines and condoms.

"How did the book come to be in your possession?"

"Well, Annie was hysterical and called her sister, who's the hairdresser of the daughter of my bridge partner."

Yadda, yadda. And the book had eventually found its way into the hands of the town's arbiter of good taste and dignity.

"Did Tim say where he got it?" he asked, betting she'd say it was from another kid at school and that all of them were rotten little sinners.

"He said he found it on the ground in the municipal parking lot, right near the school! Can you imagine?"

A bell went off in Mike's mind. He froze, his heart pounding as a strong suspicion washed over him.

Lindsey had come to the island with a case of erotic books and toys. He hadn't noticed this one in her box of tricks, but that didn't mean it wasn't hers. Had she perhaps had this one in her car, and had it then fallen out in the parking lot?

Or, wait…the laptop bag. She'd dropped it yesterday when he'd followed her out of the coffee shop. She'd been flustered and in a hurry, digging for her keys. If, for some reason she'd put the book into the case, it was possible that it had fallen out without her realizing it.

"Well, what are *you* going to do about this?"

"Mrs. Franklin, there's nothing illegal about somebody being in possession of this book. You can walk into any bookstore on the mainland and buy it."

"Well, it's illegal here!"

"No, ma'am, it isn't," he replied, knowing he was right. He'd memorized the town charter and local ordinances. There was nothing prohibiting sexy illustrations.

That was handy for old man McBride and what he had hanging up on the office wall of his gas station. Mike still hadn't gotten over the man's cartoon porn, and would never be able to watch a Disney movie again without remembering McBride's artistic talents.

Mrs. Franklin shot him a warning glare, her deep frown lines going from each side of her pursed mouth down to her jaw. "I think I'm better acquainted with the law around here than you. I want the perpetrator found and arrested."

His anger rising, he snapped, "Should we put up the stocks and have the villain displayed in the town square, too?"

The older woman jerked her head up, apparently shocked at being talked back to. Mike had always tried to remember to respect his elders—and his employers—but this was beyond ridiculous.

"You do realize you are still on probation here, Chief."

"I couldn't possibly forget it," he admitted. The couple of months remaining in his agreed-upon trial period had never seemed as long as they did right now.

"I am telling you, do your job and arrest this purveyor of smut."

He rose from his seat, leaning over his desk, his hands flat on top of it. "And I'm telling you, there's nothing illegal about this book." His eyes narrowing and his jaw clenching, he added, "There's not a damn thing you, or I, or anyone can do about it, except to remind people to please be careful not to drop their private reading materials on the ground."

That was exactly what he intended to do. Tonight, in fact. Because if Lindsey was, indeed, the owner of this manual, he needed to tell her that she'd lost it, and who had found it. He certainly wasn't going to let her walk in blind to that school Monday morning and encounter a firestorm of gossip. Knowing Mrs. Franklin, there would definitely be lots of that. Hell, she'd probably demand that the principal call an assembly so they could grill every kid to find the "pervert."

Shaking with indignation, the woman who was, technically, one of his bosses, stood up and yanked her purse against her chest. "We'll see about this."

"Careful of the step as you leave," he reminded her, crossing his arms over his chest, not budging an inch.

She opened her mouth then snapped it closed. But the thrust-out jaw and narrowed eyes said she wasn't going to let this drop.

That could be a problem, not just for him, but also for Lindsey. And for her friend Callie Parker, who sure didn't need to add a heaping of hometown scandal to what sounded like an already pretty full plate. Callie had recommended Lindsey to the school administration. If the busybodies found out Lindsey had been the one to drop what they considered "filth" close to the school grounds, they'd crucify her—and Callie, too.

So it was time he found out if his theory was true, that it was indeed Lindsey who had lost the book. It was also past time to uncover what else she'd been hiding. Because if she was *just* a schoolteacher, then he was *just* a kid playing cops-and-robbers. Maybe whatever secret she was keeping might explain why she was so reluctant to pursue any kind of relationship with him. Considering how intense their chemistry was, something big had to be holding her back.

He wanted to find out what that something was. Because he hadn't been kidding when he'd told her yesterday that he was interested in a lot more than just sex. He was falling for her, fast and hard, and he wanted Lindsey in his life any way he could get her.

Even though it was late, he couldn't let the matter wait

until morning. So, grabbing the "evidence" and dropping it into his jacket pocket, he left the station and headed for Lindsey Smith's cottage.

Frankly, he didn't know what he was hoping she'd say. That the book was not hers, and he'd be left trying to find its true owner?

Or that she'd say it was…and he'd be left wondering just how many of those erotic positions Lindsey might like to try.

With him.

WHEN LINDSEY HEARD the sharp knock on her front door, she dropped the novel she'd been reading and shot straight up in her bed. Glancing quickly at the clock and seeing it was nearly 10:00 p.m., she leaped up and grabbed her robe.

The second thing she grabbed was her cell phone. No, she didn't get great reception, but it was closer than the house phone in the kitchen.

It was kind of ridiculous that she was more jittery living here on this nice, homey little island than she'd ever been in Chicago. Perhaps it was because she just wasn't cut out to be a loner. Her new home stood on a jut of land that was at least a mile from the closest neighbor. Other than the *skree* of insects and the lapping of the waves on the nearby shore, she lived in near silence.

It grated on her nerves. She was used to traffic and shouting, to carryout, taxis, commuter trains, fast food and crowds. Not this. Not absolute quiet that, when interrupted by a knock on the door at night, seemed ominous and dangerous.

But what if it's your friendly island cop paying a call?

On one hand, that could be nice. She trusted Mike. Though she had no idea why he'd show up at her door at this time of night, she wasn't the least bit frightened of that possibility.

On the other hand, if it were Mike's obnoxious co-worker, Officer Ollie, she should definitely worry.

She'd seen the man in a few places this past week, and each time she'd gone out of her way to avoid coming face-to-face with him. Still, she'd caught his eyes on her—once in the grocery store, once in the diner. He'd tried smiling, and, when she didn't respond, had ended up narrow-eyed and angry.

Angry enough to come down here and harass me?

God, she hoped not. She had packed away her big penis-weapon in a box which was now buried in the back of her closet, so she couldn't beat him up with that.

Another knock. Still clutching the phone, she tightly tied the sash of her robe and crossed through the bedroom and the living room to the front door.

"Who is it?" she asked, not so much as lifting a hand to undo the dead bolt.

"Lindsey, it's Mike. I need to talk to you."

Relief flooding through her, she dropped the phone onto the foyer table, unlocked the door and pulled it open. "You scared me."

He offered her a half smile. "This isn't Chicago. There hasn't been a home invasion on Wild Boar for as long as anybody can remember."

"I know. It's just, the quietness is eerie. I certainly wasn't expecting somebody to knock on my door. Why did you?"

"Can I come in and explain?"

Stepping back, she gestured toward the living room. As he entered, the room seemed to shrink around him, so big was his presence.

"I see you still haven't found a permanent place for your

books," he said, nodding toward the back corner of the room, where the cartons were piled neatly against the wall.

"I won't be here that long. I figured I could just dig out the ones I want, as I want them."

He crossed his arms, leaning against the back of a tall armchair. "What about your other…package. Have you pulled out anything you wanted from that?"

The air seemed to have been sucked out of her lungs. Her mouth went dry, and she couldn't make it work to form words.

Had he really come here to talk about the sexy things that had fallen out of that box the last time they'd been together in this room? And if so, to what end?

"No, I packed it up and buried it in the bottom of my closet. It was delivered here by mistake," she admitted. "Though I was just thinking that if Officer Ollie was at my door, I might wish I had my giant rubber club handy."

He grinned. "I don't imagine he'd have even recognized it. Bullies are dickless, as a rule."

Not inside more than ninety seconds and they were already talking about sex organs. Her famous control over every personal situation had slipped away as easily as water through her fingers. That was par for the course lately, considering her professional life had slipped beyond her control, too.

Of the two, she had to admit that, right here and now, the personal one bothered her more. This man did have a knack for keeping her off guard. She wasn't used to it and didn't like it— possibly because she feared he could make her like it too much!

"Why are you here?" she finally managed to ask.

"I really am curious about that box of yours."

His husky voice and gleaming eyes made her heart flutter. Her pulse sped up, and her whole body went on alert.

Her legs quivered and she wrapped the robe tighter around herself, suddenly feeling way too vulnerable.

She wasn't scared of Mike. She was, however, scared of how quickly he made her forget all her resolutions to avoid any entanglements, especially entanglements with a man she feared she would dream about long after the hot sex was over.

"Why?"

"I'm wondering if you're missing anything out of it."

He reached into his pocket and withdrew a small book. She eyed it, recognizing the jade-green binding, and, of course, the art on the cover. Her mouth falling open, she looked from it, to him to her laptop case, which was on the coffee table. Hurrying over, she yanked it open and peered inside.

No book.

"It's possible it fell out when you dropped that case in the parking lot yesterday afternoon."

He was probably right.

God. Of course she couldn't have dropped her keys, or a wallet or some sunglasses. No. It had to be a book nobody on this island had probably ever heard of, much less read.

Except Mike. Judging by the confident gleam in his eyes, she suspected he was aware of exactly what the book contained, and had been even before this particular copy had landed in his hands.

He was bluntly sexual, so confident, so self-assured. He would not be pushed around when it came to sex. He would try new things, explore all possibilities and not be shocked by anything as simple as some graphic illustrations.

He wouldn't be told what to do. And when things grew too emotionally intense for her own comfort level, he wouldn't back off simply because she demanded it.

He won't just give you some orgasms and then leave

right away because you don't like sleeping with someone else in the room.

A leftover instinct from childhood. As a kid, she'd never been sure when she closed her eyes if she would wake up and find herself totally alone in their crappy apartment. Her parents had sometimes decided to go out and party, leaving her, even as young as age six, completely on her own.

As she got older, she preferred it when they left her alone and she tucked herself in. Going to bed *knowing* nobody would be there if she woke up during the night was much better than worrying and wondering about it.

Huh. A psychologist might speculate that was why she'd never slept an entire night in bed with a man in her whole life.

She forced all those ugly memories away. Callie had been telling her for a long time that she couldn't let her shitty past determine how she conducted herself in the present, or in the future. But putting herself—her body, her pleasure, her safety, her emotions—at the mercy of someone else, was something she'd simply never learned how to do.

Taking a deep breath, she returned to him, twisting her hands on the belt of her robe, tightening it almost painfully around her waist. "That is my book."

"Thought so."

"Thank you for giving it back to me."

"Well, some might consider it tampering with evidence. But it's really not a problem."

"I definitely wouldn't want you to get into any trouble over it." She'd hate to do anything that would jeopardize his new job and force him back to a life where he was shot at on a regular basis.

"Did it really fall out in the municipal parking lot?"

"Uh-huh."

He tossed the book to her. She caught it in one hand, glancing at it, recognizing it down to the last detail.

"And you found it after I drove away?"

The slow shake of his head increased her tension. "I'm afraid not. Someone else did the honors."

"Who?"

"A high school kid."

"Son of a bitch," she muttered.

He snickered, obviously not shocked by the schoolteacher's language. "His mother found it in his room. She passed it down the line like a hot potato until it hit the town council."

Lindsey felt as though she'd been punched. She stepped backward, almost tripping on the sash of her robe, and ran into the arm of the high-backed chair. She barely managed to stop herself from tumbling into it as she whispered, "You've got to be kidding."

"I wish I were." He shook his head, looking sad. "Mrs. Franklin was quite shocked by the, uh, pornography."

"It's not pornography," she retorted, indignant. Seeing the twinkle in his eye, she realized he agreed and that his sadness had been exaggerated.

"But it is a bit much for polite Wild Boar Island society."

She flipped open the book, eyeing the illustrations as the town council might. Tastefully drawn or not, that was a man sliding his penis into a woman whose sex was indicated with graphic slitlike lines. On the opposite page, a man's head between a woman's thighs, his exaggerated tongue stroking her mound. On the next, a woman on her knees, her lips wrapped around the tip of an erection.

The room suddenly got warmer. Lindsey swallowed, licking her lips, conscious of her quick pulse. She'd gone over these pictures plenty of times, had always viewed them with a sort of clinical detachment. They'd never left her breathless and shaky like she was now. Perhaps that was because she was being watched, oh, so closely.

She snapped the book closed and looked at Mike, noting his hooded eyes, his guarded stare.

"So, the town council, huh?" she asked, flipping her hair back over her shoulder as if she didn't really care. "Are they heating the tar and plucking the feathers?"

"I asked Mrs. Franklin if she wanted me to put the stocks in the town square."

"Ha-ha, very funny." Catching her bottom lip between her teeth, she tried to imagine how this could be resolved, but honestly didn't have a clue. "She came to you with it?"

"Yep."

"And you immediately realized it was mine?"

"I suspected as much." He walked closer. "It certainly seemed to fit in with your…collection."

His searching gaze asked a thousand questions. He was curious, obviously confused by the incongruity of the woman she appeared to be—Callie's friend, the teacher, the loner—with the woman who traveled with sex guides and cases of vibrators.

Lindsey rubbed at her eyes, wondering what to say, how much to share. She suddenly realized she liked having him here, no matter why he'd come. The last thing she wanted to do was drive him away with the truth.

But that was exactly what she had to do.

"Mike, I'm really not who you think I am."

He shrugged, completely unfazed. "If you truly believe I haven't figured that out by now, you must not rate my deductive reasoning powers too highly."

"No, I mean I'm not the nice, small-town teacher you were talking about last night."

"Did I say that? I must have been stoned."

She snorted a laugh, wondering how he could make her giggle when the topic of conversation was so important to her.

"To tell you the truth, Lindsey, I really don't care about that right now."

"*What?* What about what you said…"

"I was just trying to justify how I was feeling about you."

He had feelings? Oh boy.

"The truth is, I think about you all the time. I want to *be* with you all the time. Mrs. Franklin brought me that book, and I used it as an excuse to show up at your door at ten o'clock on a Saturday night." He smiled. "It probably could have waited, but something about you, and the *Kama Sutra*, made me get in my car and slam the pedal down."

"You don't understand. This book was a gift from Callie. She said I needed to learn how to…."

He raised a brow, waiting for her to continue, obviously mentally filling in the blank. When she didn't speak, he prompted her. "How to?"

"Be intimate," she admitted, her voice little more than a whisper.

He didn't tease her, didn't make assumptions that she automatically meant physical intimacy. Because the *Kama Sutra* was about a lot more than that. It was a little dated, a little sexist, but the entire piece had many valid things to say about loving, sensual relationships, and not all of it was about sex.

"You have trouble being intimate with people?"

She swallowed hard, trying to find the courage to admit to him what she had admitted to so few people in her life. "I have trouble *allowing* myself to be intimate with people. I don't invite them in."

"I see," he replied, coming ever closer. And then closer

still. Until his shoes nearly touched the tips of her bare toes. "The thing is, Lindsey, I think you *want* to invite me in."

She didn't have the courage to respond to that.

His long, strong leg brushed against hers, which was covered only by the silky robe. Beneath it, she wore a short, flirty nightgown that barely skimmed the tops of her thighs, and a long length of leg was revealed by the gap in the robe. The brush of his pants on her bare limbs was enough to make her weak and breathless, a little light-headed.

"Always in control," he murmured, his tone even, soothing. "Always sure of what you want and what you're doing…is that it?"

"That's some of it," she admitted, slowly nodding. She couldn't understand why her head felt full of cotton. Why was a response so hard to grasp? She may have been confused about what to say, but she was not at all confused about what she felt: *desire*.

"I suppose I should ask why. Maybe ask if that's what the box is about—you always being in control and never having to let anyone get close enough to give you what you need," he said, lifting a hand and rubbing the back of it along the V-neck of her robe. His knuckles brushed lightly across her skin, a touch as fleeting as it was evocative. Her nerve endings sang, every inch of her in tune to him.

Lindsey swallowed, feeling the excitement in the air, seeing it in his eyes, hearing it in his voice. She had no doubt he'd read that book before bringing it back, was certain he'd envisioned doing some of those things—or all of those things—with her. The tension between them had been undeniable and hot from the moment they'd met on the ferry, and they'd been shoving it away for days, with excuses and justifications.

That was all about to end, though.

Somehow, all the reasons she'd provided, all the excuses, the pithy rationale for steering clear of him, fell away. They didn't matter anymore. Because, somewhere along the way, while they'd danced this dance of yes-and-no, maybe-and-never, I-want-you-and-I-can't-have-you, she'd stopped wanting to steer clear of him. Stopped saying no, I can't have you, and never. At least in her mind.

Lindsey was a scientist, a psychologist. She understood why people did the things they did. She hadn't just been avoiding any involvement with Mike, or anyone else she met, during this "down" period in her life. She'd done the exact same thing during the "up" periods of her life, too. Even when things had been good, when her job had been rolling along and she'd had great money, a nice home, a promising future, she still hadn't allowed herself to really let down her guard with any man. Ever.

Warning Mike off hadn't been about wanting to protect her reputation or hide from the mess her life had become. It had really been about her need to stay in control.

She pushed people away. It was what she did, what she'd always done. Probably because she had gotten so used to being pushed and shoved and left to feel unimportant throughout her younger years. It had become a habit. She'd built walls long before she'd met Mike on that ferry to this place. Even though she'd sometimes lowered the walls to have sex with men, she'd never dropped them low enough to explore true intimacy, the kind that involved utter trust.

Hadn't that been why Callie had given her that book?

And how interesting that it had ended up in Mike Santori's hands, when he was the one man she'd met in, oh, forever, who she could really like. Admire. Trust.

The question was, would she trust him enough to be

vulnerable, to give up her control and allow a man to get past her defenses to the *real* her?

"Let me be blunt, Lindsey," he whispered, moving closer, until she felt his lips brushing her earlobe and his warm breaths coating her neck. "I'll want answers later. But right now, I really don't give a damn about who you are and why you travel with twenty sexy toys." His hand moved to her waist and he cupped it tightly, his fingertips stroking the curve of her bottom, tugging her even closer.

"You don't?"

"No." A tongue on her throat. "I just want to help you play with them."

She moaned softly, shocked, intrigued, so incredibly turned on by his blatant admission. He was through playing games, no longer toying—so to speak—with innuendo and suggestion.

He also wasn't finished.

"So why don't you drop that book and take me to your bedroom?"

She barely had time to let that command-masquerading-as-a-suggestion sink in before he was kissing her, his mouth hot and hard, open and hungry on hers. His tongue plunged deep, demanding everything she had, as if she was a land to be explored and he a conqueror. Every part of him made demands of her—his hands, his mouth, his words, his movements—and everything about her should have rebelled.

But nothing did. Nothing.

She simply did as he commanded. She dropped the book and melted into him, twining her arms around his neck, digging her fingers into his hair, holding him tight. She thrust her tongue against his, sucking, biting, begging. The kiss was as good as last week's, only ten times hotter, more frenzied. Maybe that was because they knew that this time he wasn't going to walk out the door with a raging hard-on, and she wasn't going to go to bed and have a wet dream about what they might have done.

This time, they would do it all.

Their bodies molded together, her softness welcoming all his wonderfully hard places. She dug her nails into his shoulder, feeling the play of muscle beneath her fingers and delighting in his raw strength. Every inch of him was masculine, the perfect counterpoint to her feminine, and she reveled in it.

"Admit how much you want this," he groaned against her mouth.

He didn't let her respond, didn't wait for her to answer, as if wanting her to admit it only to herself. Instead he thrust his tongue deep, in and out, making love to her mouth. Each stroke was accompanied by a thrust of his hips that put her in hard contact with the enormous ridge of heat tenting the front of his trousers.

She wanted that heat. Desperately. Mindlessly.

She wanted to rip his pants open and drop to her knees and put her lips and tongue on him like the illustration in that book. She longed to taste him until he came in her mouth, leaving him bone-dry and weak. And after she swallowed down some of that power, taking it for herself, maybe then she could be sure he was just as vulnerable, just as helpless to his body's demands as she was right now.

But did she really care about evening scores or jockeying for power? No. Right now she just wanted to suck his cock.

Lindsey quivered, realizing she was crossing over some boundary here. She was out of her mind with want.

She was out of control.

Whatever he wanted from her, he could have, if only he'd stop this almost-painful need, slake her dreadful thirst. And he was aware of just how much he could take; he hadn't waited for an answer because it had been a mere formality.

He knew what she wanted. What she needed. And he would give it to her.

He yanked at the tie of her robe and pushed it open. He put his strong hands around her midriff, sliding them up to cup her breasts. His thumbs flicked up to trace her hard nipples, pressing against the pale blue satin of her nightie, and her legs almost buckled.

"Oh, yes, touch me. More, Mike," she ordered.

His hands immediately dropped, moving away, tormenting her.

Because she'd ordered?

His kiss became harder, insistent, demanding that she give herself over to him.

Stop trying to control. Stop making demands.

Trust him. Let him. And let yourself.

She hesitated, part of her rebelling. The urge to try to gain the edge, to turn the tables, whispered inside her. But somehow she knew if she did, she'd be the one who suffered. Maybe they'd still have great sex tonight, but tomorrow, she would be able to convince herself he was just like everyone else she'd ever slept with. A man who didn't mind doing what she told him to, as long as he got his rocks off.

Mike's not that man.

He could never be.

And if she pushed him to be that man, she might not have great sex with him tonight—or ever. Because he'd just turn around and walk out the door.

She couldn't bear that. No matter what it cost her or how it might hurt, she couldn't let him go without submitting to at least one remarkable night with him.

All she had to do was let him into every part of her, not just her body. All she had to do was surrender.

Just surrender.

He softened the kiss, cajoling her, seducing her. He continued to touch her with long, teasing strokes that were never quite enough.

Surrender.

Finally, she did. She trusted him.

"Anything you want, Mike," she whispered into his mouth, whimpering, dying. "Any way you want it."

He pulled away, looking down at her, masculine satisfaction written all over his face. His eyes glittered, the pupils dark with want, and a confident smile tugged at that incredible mouth. "Are you absolutely sure? Because I won't stand for barriers. I'll plow right through them."

Swallowing, she nodded, both scared and incredibly turned on by his self-assurance. He wasn't threatening her, he was promising her. She only had to let down her defenses and he'd push through until she felt so good she wouldn't remember her own name, much less her silly objections.

"I'm sure."

"Okay then."

He stroked her slowly, sliding his hands back up to cup her breasts again. But he focused only on her face, watching her intently, as if to ensure she really was ready to let him lead the way.

Lindsey gasped when he pushed the robe off her shoulders, pulled the spaghetti straps of her nightgown down and peeled the silky fabric from her chest. She hissed when his thumbs scraped over her taut nipples, sensation rocketing through her. She moaned when he finally kissed his way down her throat and licked the top curves of her breasts.

And when he finally covered one puckered nipple with his mouth and sucked, hard, she gave a little groan.

Heat burst through her; she truly was on fire, mindless, desperate to know what he'd do next but not asking, not interfering. Just taking.

He sucked her, tweaked her, exploring her breasts with his hands and his mouth until she was sagging into the arm of the chair. Then he kissed his way back up to her mouth and pulled her to her feet. But he didn't keep her there.

Not letting the kiss end, he picked her up by the hips, holding her bottom in his big, strong hands. She instinctively wrapped her legs around his hips, almost crying at the sensation of cupping that long, hard ridge of flesh between her thighs. She ground against it, desperate for the pressure, the strength, and whimpered as her sex swelled and moistened, pulsing with electric fire.

"God, yes," she groaned. "Please, I need to…"

"No," he ordered, lifting her higher so her sex was pressed against his waist, removed from that connection she craved. "You don't take it—I give it to you."

"But…"

"I said no," he growled. "Not yet. Not until I say so."

She sucked in a shocked breath, staring into his face. He didn't smile, didn't wink, didn't tell her he was joking. He merely held her stare, laying down his conditions.

Mike didn't want merely her surrender. He wanted her total and complete submission.

The modern woman within her screamed in frustration.

The sexual being within her purred in anticipation.

Being free to do nothing but feel. No thoughts, no plans, no reactions…just sensation. Pleasure. The very concept scared her. It thrilled her. It overwhelmed her. It intoxicated her. She couldn't think, could barely breathe; she could only give in to her true desire. And her true desire was something that would have stunned her just ten days ago.

"All right, Mike. For tonight, at least, you'll be in charge. I'll do whatever you tell me to do."

7

THERE HADN'T BEEN much doubt in Mike's mind of exactly what Lindsey wanted and needed, even if she didn't know it herself. But until she actually agreed, he'd held his breath.

The moment the words left her lips, he released that breath with a self-satisfied groan. "You won't regret it," he promised her, intending to keep that promise no matter what it took.

Not giving her any more time to reconsider, he headed for her room. Kicking the door open so he could carry her through it, he crossed to the bed, tossing her down upon it.

Lindsey landed amongst a pile of pillows, half reclining. She was now covered only by a skimpy pair of panties and a tiny, wispy light blue nightgown that was pulled down low on her breasts, not even covering one well-sucked nipple. The fabric floated up over her hips when she landed, so now it covered only her middle.

He didn't follow her down, instead he stood by the bed, looking down at her. She reached toward one of her spaghetti straps—to pull it back up or push it all the way off? Didn't matter. He hadn't said she could.

"Ah-ahh," he tsked. "I didn't tell you to do that."

Her hand froze; she eyed him with uncertainty. A beat. Then she lowered her hand onto the bed. Obeying.

Though he knew she was still unsure about this, her eyes glowed and her face was flushed with hunger. Her kiss-reddened lips trembled. Those beautiful nipples he'd suckled were hard and moist, and he'd lay money she wanted to lift her own hand to tweak them, just so she could have a moment's satisfaction.

She didn't move, however. She merely watched. Waited.

"Good girl."

"I'm not calling you *master,*" she said with a tiny, playful smile, though her words sounded unsure—forced.

"You will if I tell you to," he said, his voice low, silky, brooking no disobedience. He reached down and pushed her hair away from her face, brushing his thumb over her lips. "Won't you, Lindsey?"

She blinked, her cheeks reddening, from anger? From excitement? Was a war going on behind her green eyes? He couldn't be sure, not until her tongue flicked at his thumb, as if she simply had to taste him. And then she slowly nodded.

He had no intention of making her call him master; however, she'd just agreed that he could. Not forever, certainly not outside this bedroom. But here and now, oh yes, he could, and she knew it. *Progress.*

He began to unbutton his shirt, pulling it free of his pants. She watched closely, her breaths growing audible as she parted her lips and inhaled over them. When he undid his cuffs, pulled the shirt off and dropped it to the floor, she groaned, approval and hunger warring in her expression. Her hips thrust the tiniest bit, indicating she had no control over her body's reaction. She wanted him desperately. Wanted to touch him and explore him, as he wanted to explore her.

But not yet.

"Take that off," he ordered, nodding toward her nightie.

She didn't refuse, didn't tell him he forgot to say please. Lindsey was getting caught up in this. She was *enjoying* it.

Crossing her arms over her breasts, already mostly revealed to his hungry gaze, she pushed the straps down, pulling her arms free, and letting the gown float into a puddle on her lap. Her breasts were works of art, round and full, but not too heavy. He could still taste those rosy nipples on his tongue.

He watched as she pushed the gown down over her hips, then her thighs, until she could kick it out of the way. It fluttered to the floor near his feet, a wisp of a thing, simple but so very erotic when it was taken off.

He stared, rubbing his hand on his jaw, noting the scratch of his five o'clock shadow. For a long moment, he looked at her, picking out all the places on her body where she'd soon feel that scratch. Those breasts, that throat, that stomach and the hollow beneath it, right above her pelvis.

And oh, those legs and what lay between them.

"The panties, too."

She licked her lips, apparently a little uncertain about stripping naked while he just stood there watching.

"Do it."

Her eyes flared, but not in annoyance. She was excited as hell. It rolled off her in waves, electric and thrilling.

Lindsey might not have understood she wanted this, but he had.

Ever since he'd met her, he'd caught mentions and hints about how much she needed to maintain control. She'd made it clear she didn't let down her guard, that she made rules and set boundaries. Her own best friend had tried to teach her how to accept real, genuine intimacy by giving her that book.

All of which just told him one thing: she needed to be fucked by somebody who wasn't scared to say no to her.

Somebody who would not let her hide behind her quick humor or stop things from going beyond her predetermined acceptable point of intimacy. The decision had to be taken out of her hands so she would just experience this, rather than having to orchestrate every aspect of it.

"Did you not hear me?" he said, his tone holding an edge, his eyes on that pretty triangle of silk between her thighs.

Reaching for the elastic hem, she wriggled the underwear off. As she pushed the panties down her legs, she bent forward a little, her long red hair falling down onto her lap, covering the parts of her he most wanted to see. She plucked the lacy bit of nothing off and tossed it away to land with her nightgown, then looked up at him. That long hair still covered too much, including her breasts.

"Push your hair back."

She lifted her hands, twined her fingers through the long, silky strands then moved them back over her shoulders, revealing those breasts again. *Perfect.*

"Lie down."

Moving slowly, she did, reclining on the pile of cushions. Twisting her hair, she let it fall across the pillows in a vivid red splash against the pillowcase. One hand remained on the bed, relaxed and vulnerable, the other rested on her flat stomach.

His attention, however, was drawn a little bit lower.

He ground his teeth, clenching his jaw to hold himself together. That tuft of red curls at the apex of her thighs was small and angled, a little arrow pointing down toward the lips of her sex, concealed between her coyly closed legs.

"Let me see *all* of you."

This time, she didn't hesitate. She was captured by the

excitement. Bending one knee, she slid her foot up, letting her legs fall open. He groaned at the sight of that erotically smooth flesh between them; the curls were only at the very top, just for decoration.

Such pretty decoration.

But damn, was it pretty without them.

He'd never been with a woman who waxed quite so thoroughly. The thought of burying his mouth in her, licking into those juicy crevices, finding her hard little clit and working it with his tongue until she screamed, made his cock ache.

"You are *beautiful*," he said.

"Thank you," she murmured, looking pleased by the compliment. It certainly couldn't have been the first time she'd heard it—the woman was drop-dead gorgeous. Then again, considering he suspected she never let any guy really glimpse the real her, maybe she didn't hear it all that often, beyond the superficial pickup lines.

"Beautiful," he repeated, because it needed to be said twice.

He reached for his belt, unfastened it and pulled it out quickly. The leather cracked as it left the loops of his pants. Lindsey stiffened, her hands fisting, and he knew what thought had flashed across that brilliant mind.

He hated that her thoughts had instinctively gone to such a place. Had someone abused her? Was that why she found it so impossible to give herself over and trust someone completely?

"I'd *never* hurt you," he assured her, sure she'd already accepted that, deep down, but might need to hear it anyway.

She nodded, swallowing visibly. He noted the reaction, more sure of his suspicion. Somewhere along the way, someone *had* hurt her, maybe not physically, but emotionally she'd been conditioned to expect the worst.

The very idea infuriated him, but he definitely didn't want her to sense anger in him and tense up. So he forced it away and gave her a sexy, self-assured smile as he reached for the waistband of his pants.

The tension left her as she watched him, and she almost cooed as he unbuttoned, then unzipped his khakis. He had to pull the material away to get the zipper down over his rigid cock. He'd never been this hard; the brush of his own fingers through the cotton of his shorts made him flinch.

He didn't drop the pants, letting them hang low on his hips. He did reach for the elastic waistband of his boxer briefs, though, pulling them down a little. Never tearing his eyes off her, he grabbed his dick, big and throbbing, letting her see how much he wanted her. Stroking himself lazily, he acknowledged that her hands would be so much better, but he wasn't yet ready to let her do anything but lie there and take what he planned to give her.

She devoured him with her stare, so approving—wanting—and his own hunger dug into him even more brutally. It clawed at him, made him almost desperate to rip off his clothes and just take her until neither of them could think, much less move.

But that wasn't how this was going to go down.

Hmm. Speaking of which…

He sat on the corner of the bed, touching her bare foot, trailing his fingers up her long leg. Lindsey's eyes fell closed and she arched her back. Her skin was incredibly soft against his hand, and it got even softer the higher he went. Her thighs were exquisite.

As he reached the top of one and moved his hand inward, brushing his fingertips through that tiny landing patch of curls, she trembled. He knew what she wanted, what she craved. He could see the pearly tip of her clit, and the glisten of arousal on her sex—she was dying for him to make the touch ever so much more intimate.

She didn't say a word, didn't make a single demand, didn't even thrust up toward his hand. She was relaxed now; she trusted him, assured he wouldn't leave her high and dry. Willing to let him set the pace.

He would not disappoint her.

He bent to press his mouth on the hollow just inside her hip, tracing his tongue across the skin, tasting a faint tinge of salt. *Sweat.* He was making her hot. Maybe next time, he'd use an ice cube to cool her off.

Still driving her mad with those soft strokes in the hollow just above her sex, he began to kiss his way up her body. He nibbled at her hip bone, licked the indentation of her waist, detouring over to dip his tongue into her belly button. She quivered beneath him, and when he glanced up, he found her eyes closed and her mouth shaking. That glorious hair surrounded her like a halo, and her flushed face had never looked more lovely.

He continued kissing, stroking, tasting, until he reached her breasts. He licked the base of one, nibbled the top of the other, but didn't go near her nipples.

She was still silent, but her hands dug at the sheets and her legs had gone a little stiff.

"Do you want more?"

She nodded.

"Put your hands up onto the headboard and hold on."

She did as he commanded, gripping the slats. "Like this?"

"Yes. Don't let go. Hold on like you're *handcuffed* there."

A gasp told him he'd shocked her. "You wouldn't…"

"As long as you hold on tight, I won't have to."

She stared at him, wondering, assessing.

Had he pushed too far? *Come on, Lindsey, give in. Trust me.*

Finally, after an eternity, she licked her lips. "I won't let go, but if I do, use a scarf from the bureau. Your cuffs might damage the wood on the bed."

Relieved, turned on, overwhelmed with excitement, and, honestly, proud of her for continuing to do something he knew she had never done before, he could only smile and nod. "Now, where were we?"

"I think you were going to pay attention to my nipples."

"You think so?"

"Uh-huh."

"Maybe if you *beg* me to."

She didn't even hesitate, her eyes dark and dreamy and her voice throbbing. "Please, Mike. I'm begging you, please suck my nipples. I need it, badly."

He immediately complied, relieving the tension for both of them, since he'd been just as desperate to taste her as she'd been to be tasted. He covered one tip and sucked it deeply into his mouth, tweaking her other breast, plucking, giving her a little pain that would only increase the pleasure.

She groaned and hissed and arched into him. Her hips thrust instinctively, and he knew she'd reached the point of near desperation.

He couldn't torture her, couldn't ignore the raw need in her. Keeping his mouth on her breast, he moved his hand down, scraping the tip of his finger on her sensitive clit.

"Oh, God," she cried. But she didn't let go of the headboard.

He stroked her, teased her, building things ever higher. Wanting to watch her reach the heights, he stopped suckling her and lifted his head, focusing on that perfect face,

Leslie Kelly 135

racked with pleasure that verged on agony, consumed by the fire he was building but unable to put it out.

How could he not give her what she *wasn't* asking for?

He slid his hand lower, his fingertips gliding through the slick, feminine flesh. Finding her wet center, he thrust a finger into her tight core. She bucked up, panting. He stroked, in and out, giving her another finger, increasing the pressure while still toying with her clit with his thumb.

She jerked and rolled her head back and forth on the pillow, losing herself to sensation. She was almost over the edge, but he wasn't quite ready to let her go, so he pulled his fingers away.

"Are you *kidding* me?" she snarled.

"Wait until I can catch you."

"I'm not falling."

"You're about to," he promised, moving down between her splayed legs. He pushed them farther apart, draped one over his shoulder and gazed at that swollen, slick beauty.

Bending to her, he covered her with his mouth and thrust his tongue deep, licking into her.

She screamed in shocked delight.

Ignoring her, Mike continued to make love to her with his tongue, only moving up to pay attention to her clit when he was sure she was on the verge of exploding. He sucked the pearly little button into his mouth, flicked it, toyed with it and fingered her again, bringing her higher. So very high, until they were both shaking with the intensity.

"Lindsey?" he muttered against her sex.

"What?"

"You can fall now."

He put his mouth on her again, and she did as she was told. She'd climbed to the heights and now she leaped off, a climax slamming into her so hard her body shuddered.

Her toes curled, her hands clenched the headboard, her skin shone with a rosy glow.

While she rode it out, looking the epitome of sensual woman, he got up and stripped out of the rest of his clothes. He grabbed a condom from the pocket of his pants—he'd put it there this week, after he'd met her on the ferry, and was very glad to have followed the impulse.

Lindsey was still quivering, her gasps slowly turning into sighs, though her eyes remained closed. She was a limp, boneless heap. Her thighs were open, her breasts red and marked by his mouth.

She looked utterly wanton. And he had to be in her or he would die.

He moved back between her legs and her eyes flew open.

"Can I please hold you?" she asked.

Nodding solemnly, he stayed still as she reached for him, sliding her fingers into his hair, holding him tight, like she was afraid he'd go somewhere. *As if.*

"That was amazing," she said.

"I know."

He dropped his face to hers and caught her mouth in a hungry kiss, even as he pulled one of her legs up around his hip and opened her even wider for his ultimate possession. He nudged against her wet heat, his cock sinking between her folds and then into her tight, slick core.

She wrapped around him, took him inch by inch, arched her hips up in welcome. And the deeper he sank, the more certain he was that he'd fallen and landed in heaven.

"Oh, yes," she cried, nipping at his jaw, raking her nails down his back. He didn't return to their game, didn't tell her what to do. This was elemental—primal. Instinct had taken them both over and they were helpless to do anything but come together in a storm of need.

She tightened her leg around his hip, urging him deeper, and he was unable to resist driving all the way into her with a powerful thrust. He sank deep, until he was seated to the hilt.

She let out a little scream.

"Are you all right?"

"No," she said, breathless, hoarse. "But I'm all messed up in the very best way."

That didn't make sense, but he understood it anyway. She'd let down her guard, broken her own rules. Lindsey had opened up to him in every way she possibly could. Because of that trust, that confidence in him, he was sure she was savoring the same amazing, life-changing pleasure he was, as the two of them rocked and thrust, gave and took.

He was possessed by her, wanting to possess her back. He didn't feel like he could ever get into her deeply enough, but he tried. Oh, God, he tried. Grabbing her leg, he pushed it higher until it draped over his shoulder, and she gasped as he claimed that much more of her.

They rocked hard, slaves to their bodies. The tension spiraled out of control. She urged him on, groaning, begging, thrusting. Until finally, with that little back-of-the-throat cry he'd recognize for the rest of his life, she came again.

Which was enough to bring him right along with her.

LINDSEY WOKE WITH a surprised start, not sure what had awakened her from the amazingly hot dream she'd been having.

It took her a second to figure out where she was and to understand the truth: it had not been a dream. The weight of a strong, masculine arm draped across her waist, the beat of a heart against her shoulder and the soft, even exhalations against her temple proved it.

Everything came flooding back, from the minute he'd knocked on the door until the moment they'd both been gripped in the crazy passion that had them pounding, breathless, sweaty and insane.

And the rest. God, the rest of it. *Did I really submit to his every demand?*

Yes. She had.

She closed her eyes again, letting herself remember every moment, letting herself believe. It hadn't been a fantasy creeping up from the inner recesses of her mind, some longing she'd never known she felt. She really had surrendered herself, body, mind and spirit, to a man she'd only met a week ago.

A man who now slept with her in her bed. A man with whom *she* had fallen asleep.

That shocked her, and she blinked, glancing over at the bedside clock. It was 2:00 a.m. After the amazing sex, she'd fallen asleep, as if it was an everyday occurrence. He'd obviously gotten up to turn off the lights and rejoined her, holding her as tightly in his sleep as he had when awake.

He'd warned her he would, yet Mike had no idea he'd broken down yet another of her barriers. She lay very still in the circle of his arms, feeling the scrape of his leg, the warmth of his skin, the press of his half-aroused sex against her hip.

It took her only a moment to realize she was waiting for the panic to set in, and another to acknowledge that it hadn't.

She was okay. Actually, she was fine. Good. Thrilled even.

Because, just remembering the way she'd delivered herself into his hands, and how seriously he'd taken that responsibility, was enough to give her not only reassurance, but chills of satisfaction.

Some of her patients had confessed they liked being tied up, even spanked. She'd had her own opinions about that, essentially thinking, *No way in hell would I ever do it.* But she'd always been able to ignore her own reactions and focus on helping her patients understand why they made the choices they did. They talked a lot about why they wanted what they wanted, and how to ensure their relationships were healthy ones... Even ones with spankings.

All that meant she *should* be able to understand why she'd made the choice she had made last night. The truth flitted around the edges of her mind, not quite coming into focus. Undoubtedly, it was partly to do with her own physical needs...and partly to do with the man who'd demanded the right to fulfill them. Beyond that, she couldn't put the entire picture together. She only knew it had been the best sex of her life and that she would never regret it.

"You're awake," he whispered. She hadn't even realized he was no longer sleeping, and the voice coming out of the darkness startled her for a second.

As if sensing that, he tightened his arm around her, pulling her even closer, and pressed a kiss on her forehead.

"I can't believe I fell asleep right away," she admitted.

"You obviously needed it. I doubt you've slept well this week. New place, new bed and all that."

"Maybe." She turned to face him, lifting her leg and sliding it over his. The position pressed them that much closer together, and a shiver of delight went through her. She felt him hardening, second by second. With a shimmy and a thrust, she could have him inside her again.

She wanted that very much, but there was the issue of birth control to consider. She hadn't bothered to bring her diaphragm to the island, never in a million years thinking she'd require it. Mike had taken care of things last night, thank God, but unless he came *doubly* prepared, they were going to be out of luck as far as that went, at least until tomorrow.

Of course, there were other things they could do.

Other pleasures to explore.

"Maybe you just wore me out," she said, licking her lips as she imagined what else she'd like to do to him and with him.

"It's mutual." He ran his hand down her side, reaching her hip and tugging her even closer against him. He was as hard as a rock now, his cock nestled in the folds of her sex, which was slick and welcoming. But he made no effort to go further.

"No more condoms, huh?" she asked.

He sighed heavily. "Nope. You?"

"Nary a one. And I don't have anything else."

"Well, damn, so much for believing you were a Girl Scout."

"I take it you weren't a Scout, either?"

"Hey, I came prepared for round one."

True. She didn't ask him why. She honestly didn't want to know whether he always went around with a condom in his pocket, or if he'd put it in there only after he'd met her. One answer might depress her, the other might annoy her. So it was best not to ask the question.

"I don't suppose there's an all-night pharmacy around here where we could stock up for rounds two through ten?"

"First, even if there were an all-night pharmacy, I'm not sure it would be wise for the police chief and the new schoolteacher to walk in there at two in the morning and buy rubbers."

"Maybe not," she said with a heavy sigh that wasn't

quite feigned. Remembering what he'd said, she asked, "What's second?"

"Second...*ten?*" he said, half laughing, half groaning.

"Oh, come on. You're young, you're strong. Where's all that hot Italian blood I've heard about?" she teased.

"At this particular moment," he said as he leaned forward to nuzzle her neck, "it's all in my cock. But there's not much I can do about that, now, is there?"

"Sure there is," she said, arching back so he could trace his tongue down to the hollow of her throat. His breath was warm against her skin, his lips soft and tender. "All you have to do is *tell* me what you want."

He lifted his head and stared at her, his dark eyes gleaming in the shadowy room, lit only by a hint of moonlight spilling in the front window. His hair was tousled, his jaw shadowed, his expression *hungry.* Lindsey was certain she'd never seen a sexier sight in her life.

"Not ask you?" he said, catching her emphasis.

She stroked a muscular shoulder, scraping her nails lightly across that smooth skin. "I'm finding I take direction better than I thought I ever would."

"What if I directed you to go get something out of your toy box for us to play with?"

Shivering, shocked by the excitement that rushed through her, she said, "Well, you'd have to give me a few minutes to dig it out of the closet."

"Why don't you do that?" he said, kissing her collarbone, his hand stroking her thigh. "Pick out your favorite."

"I don't have one. I was serious when I said I've never used any of them."

He paused, his hand staying where it was, and lifted his head until they were face-to-face. "Yeah. About that...?"

She understood what he was asking. They'd avoided the topic for a week, she'd never come out and told him what she really did for a living, or why she had a vast collection of sexual aids. She owed him an explanation, especially after what had happened with the *Kama Sutra* found in the parking lot.

Steeling herself for his reaction, whatever it might be, she said, "In my real life, I'm a counselor."

"Like, at a high school?"

That was probably a logical assumption for him to make, but she laughed lightly. "I mean, a psychological counselor. A therapist. I work—I mean, I *hope* I still work—at a health-and-wellness center in downtown Chicago."

Mike sat up straight, the sheets falling onto his lap. She eyed that big, broad chest, with its light sprinkling of dark, wiry hair. He was *so* nice to look at. The man was amazingly handsome during the day, but he was made to wear night.

Right now, though, he'd been thoroughly distracted from all the things he did so well during the night. Gaping down at her, he asked, "Are you serious?"

"Yes."

"Are you a doctor?"

"Not an M.D., but yes, a psychologist."

"What on earth are you doing working as a teacher?"

Lindsey sighed as she realized the mood had definitely been broken. It appeared they were going to have to talk instead of getting to the naughty things she wanted to do to him.

"I'm on a leave of absence," she admitted. "But the timing was perfect because of Callie's situation. I've tried hard not to let anybody find out who I am. I don't think the therapist-moonlighting-as-teacher thing would go over very well here."

"Definitely not."

She caught her lip between her teeth, eyeing him apologetically. "That's one reason I tried to avoid getting involved with you. If this all comes crashing down, and you get caught in the cross fire, you could lose your job, especially with that whole stupid incident with the book. I'd be devastated if you were fired because of me."

"I won't be."

"I'm so very thankful that you got out of the Chicago P.D. before you got seriously hurt."

Not saying anything, he lifted a hand and rubbed a scar on the base of his throat, as if by habit. She'd noticed it before—she'd kissed it a few hours ago.

Understanding, she murmured, "Is that a reminder of your last job?"

He nodded. "Yeah. Just my bad luck to run into a desperate gangbanger with a long knife, who was out to earn his stripes."

An inch closer to his jugular, and he would have bled out. She didn't have to be an M.D. to know that.

Lindsey had to close her eyes and swallow hard to give herself a moment to come to grips with that. He could so easily have been killed, could have, without a doubt, ceased to exist before she'd ever gotten the chance to know him. That realization stunned and horrified her, and again, she wondered if she'd made a mistake getting involved with him. Because, God forbid he ever had to return to that life, especially because of a stupid job!

Finally, she replied, "Actually, I think it's your good luck that his knife wasn't longer or his aim wasn't better."

"Forget about all that. It's in the past," he said. Then he went back to her explanation. "What's this leave of absence about?"

"It's about getting me out of the way because I'm a liability."

"What?"

"My employers asked me to go. They are calling it a leave of absence, but the truth is, it's more like probation. I have to keep my nose clean, stay out of the papers, not draw any unpleasant attention that would reflect badly on the center. Maybe then they'll welcome me back."

"Assholes," he said, lying down again to draw her close.

She didn't say anything for a moment, a little stunned at his reaction. There had been no, "What did you do?" No, "Why?" just an indictment of whoever had done something to hurt her.

Oh, this man was special in so many ways. So loyal and so trustworthy. Which was why she decided to trust him and just reveal everything.

"I work for an extremely conservative practice. Very old school and stodgy. Unfortunately, the media got ahold of some excerpts of my dissertation on female orgasms and made a big joke out of it, putting my name, and the center's, through the tabloid wringer."

He shook his head, as if clearing it to understand. "Women's… Wait, what kind of counselor are you?"

Too late to retreat now.

"I'm a sex therapist. I specialize in female sexual disorders."

He shot up again. Then, as if that wasn't enough, he jumped out of the bed, standing naked beside it, gaping down at her. His brows shot up as his eyes rounded. His mouth fell open, snapped shut then opened again, as if he didn't know what to say. Finally he managed, "You're joking."

"No, I'm not."

He was clearly having a hard time wrapping his mind around it. "You teach people how to have sex?"

"Not exactly. It's more about helping patients—primarily women—understand their bodies and figure out why they make the choices they do when it comes to their sex lives. That's why I have all the toys, by the way."

He nodded slowly. "Like pharmacies giving out free drugs to doctors so they'll prescribe the drugs to their patients."

"Exactly!" she exclaimed, glad he'd understood so quickly. "I have definitely recommended vibrators to some of my non-orgasmic patients."

He swiped a hand through his hair, shaking his head, still a little shell-shocked. She supposed it was a bit much to take in, since he'd viewed her as the small-town teacher she'd been portraying.

"Mike, are you all right?"

She knew what his problem was. It was the same problem all the men she slept with had when they found out what she did. They were intimidated, thinking they were having sex with an "expert," wondering if they were being judged or evaluated. She understood, which was why, in the past, she rarely told her lovers what she did for a living. Considering her relationships rarely lasted long, and never got to the point of true intimacy, it had never been a problem keeping that detail secret.

Mike, though, had already barreled through those defenses, just as he'd warned her he would. Revealing her profession hadn't been just about making him understand about the toys. She also wanted him to know her—really know her—the way few people did.

When he didn't answer, she said, "Are *we* all right?"

She wasn't sure what "we" meant yet, but she realized she would not be satisfied with just one night with the man. The timing and location were beyond bad; nothing had changed in that regard. The only thing that *had* changed was that they both now knew how worth the effort a hot, secret affair would be.

"We're fine," he said, sitting on the edge of the bed, looking down at her. He reached out and brushed her hair back off her cheek, the caress tender and gentle. "But I'm glad you didn't tell me that before. Having sex with a sex therapist? Talk about something to give a guy performance anxiety!"

She purred. "Baby if that's your standard performance, you have nothing to be anxious about. Ever."

A pleased, self-satisfied grin tugged at his lips. "Yeah?"

"Definitely. That was worthy of a standing ovation. I will be demanding an encore."

He ran his fingers over her belly, gliding them up to caress the under-curve of a breast. "How many curtain calls?"

Growing breathless as his fingers danced across her skin, she murmured, "I believe the number we discussed was ten."

"After a trip to the pharmacy." He sighed. "Tomorrow."

"Or maybe your place tonight? I assume the one you bought came with brothers and sisters in the box?"

He nodded. "But I live right downtown in an apartment over one of the antique stores."

Oh. Talk about a lack of privacy.

"So I guess we're just going to have to find something else to do right now," he said as he traced a line up to her nipple and stroked it with his fingertip.

She gasped, loving the connection. But Mike had already done a lot for her tonight, and she was definitely ahead of him on the orgasm-meter.

A few hours ago, she'd been consumed by the idea of

tasting him—of taking him into her mouth and sucking him into incoherence. Now seemed the perfect time to do exactly that. "Was there something you wanted to tell me?"

His expression said he didn't understand.

"About what you want me to do?" She caressed his stomach, lowering her fingers to tangle them into the thatch of hair at the base of his sex. Encircling him with her hand, she stroked, up and down, and leaned forward to scrape her tongue across the seam of his lips, silently letting him know where else she'd like to lick him.

She heard his breaths quicken as he caught her meaning. "I'm not sure that's something any man should ever *tell* a woman to do."

She kissed her way down his rough jaw, still stroking him, occasionally dropping her hand lower to fondle the tight, vulnerable sacs below his erection.

"Okay, so you won't order me. So do you want to tell me what you'd *like* me to do?" She squeezed him tighter, rubbing her thumb across the tip of his cock, where a bit of moisture dripped. Lifting her hand to her mouth, she licked it off, her eyes never leaving his.

"Yeah. I'll tell you."

She smiled, triumphant, sure of what he would say.

"I'd like for you to sit on my face."

Her turn to gasp. That was *not* what she'd expected him to say. "But I want to…"

"You can absolutely suck my cock. At the same time." His tone was as wicked as his expression. "I'm a multi-tasker."

"Mmm," she moaned, understanding what he wanted. Her whole body went warm and weak, moisture flooding her sex as she pictured it. She'd talked about this position with her patients, had taught it, even, but she'd never actually done it. This was the kind of intimacy long-term lovers engaged in, and her relationships usually didn't last that long. Leave it to Mike to blow all those expectations away and suggest something so deliciously wicked on their very first night together.

Reaching for her jaw, he angled her face toward his and caught her mouth in a hot, hungry kiss. His tongue thrust deeply against hers, exploring her as if he hadn't just kissed her to within an inch of her life a few hours ago.

Their mouths still joined, he rolled onto his back, pulling her on top of him. Lindsey rubbed against him, loving the feel of that powerful heat between her legs, but wanting it now in her mouth.

When the kiss ended, she didn't wait for him to make the next move. She turned around, maybe a little unsure, but also very aroused, exploring his hard, muscular body as she went. Mike took hold of her hips, pulling her back until she knelt, her knees on either side of his face.

"God, this is gorgeous," he muttered before bringing her to his mouth and licking deep.

It was, as before, incredible. He used his tongue and lips to build an inferno inside her, and she was determined to make him just as fiery.

She lay down on top of him, taking his cock into her hand, marveling at its size and silky texture. The first brush of her lips on its tip caused him to flinch, and she smiled, glad she made him as crazy as he was making her. Flicking her tongue out, she tasted him, wetting him, then covered the engorged tip and sucked him into her mouth.

He groaned against her thigh, an unintelligible expression of lust, heat and satisfaction. Knowing he was savoring everything she did, she took more of him, and still more. Every stroke of her tongue was matched by one of his, and she honestly couldn't say which was more delightful. The intensity overwhelmed her, but she never wanted it to stop.

The whole thing was so incredibly intimate—so erotic—that it was only a few minutes before a climax started rising in her. Not wanting to go there alone, she tightened her grip on the base of his shaft. She stroked him harder while her mouth worked him into a frenzy. He was groaning his pleasure against her sex as he licked and sucked her clit, bringing her ever closer to nirvana.

Finally, when she knew she couldn't hold out another moment, she felt his body tense and jerk.

"Lindsey, you don't have to…"

He was giving her the opportunity to pull away. *Fat chance.*

Sucking him as deeply as she could, she felt the slick fluid gush into her throat, salty, musky and hot. The carnality of it, combined with the incredible things he was doing to her with his mouth, pushed her right over the top, too.

Afterward, spent and satisfied, she kissed his flaccid penis, licking away the last of his juices, and turned around. She collapsed onto his chest, and Mike immediately wrapped his arms around her, pulling her to him for a slow, sultry kiss.

When it ended, she rested her head on his shoulder. Their breathing slowed, their heartbeats normalized—she could feel his against her chest.

Reality returned, and with it, sanity.

What had they done? Somehow she had to reestablish her boundaries, create some distance. They both had too much at stake not to.

Clearly not experiencing the same doubts, Mike rubbed a lazy hand down her back. "I've got to say, Lindsey, if that was number two, I just can't wait to find out what three through ten are like."

8

"TELL ME ABOUT this Thinkgasm thing."

Sitting across from Lindsey at the empty coffee shop at six-thirty one weekday morning, Mike had waited until he was sure the owner was in the kitchen, out of earshot, before asking his question.

That was a good thing, because his lover almost hacked up a lung coughing over the mouthful of coffee she'd just sipped. He leaned across the table and patted her on the back. "Sorry, I didn't mean to make you choke."

She got control of herself and quickly scanned the shop. "Are you crazy?"

"There's nobody else here." There probably would be in another fifteen or twenty minutes, when the other teachers and high school students started drifting in for their morning charge-ups. But for now they were entirely alone.

Lindsey had been working very hard to get her classes up to speed for their end-of-the-year exams. She'd told him that during the first two weeks of Callie's surprise maternity leave, the inexperienced sub had done nothing but show movies with vaguely scientific themes—like *Jurassic Park*. So Lindsey always went in to the school superearly to get on top of the day's work. She might not be a teacher by vocation, but she was dedicated and very serious about her temporary job. Just something else to admire about her.

Usually, she got her coffee to go. Mike knew that, which was why he'd made his own stop here as soon as he'd gotten off his overnight shift. He'd been waiting for her when she walked in, his smile a challenge, his offer to sit down and have coffee with him an invitation she couldn't refuse. Risky, but since the place was deserted, she had agreed.

"Now, Thinkgasms?"

"You've been searching me on Google."

"Did you really think I wouldn't?"

She ran the tip of her index finger along the rim of her mug. "Actually, I'm surprised it took you this long. It's been ten whole days since you found out who I really am."

Ten days. Was that all? Seemed as if he'd known her—been her lover—far longer than that. She'd become so much a part of his life, he had trouble remembering how he'd spent his spare time on the island before her arrival.

"You do a good job distracting me." He smiled over his cup, letting her see the warm appreciation in his stare. Damn, he wanted her. They'd only been able to grab an hour together yesterday, between the end of her workday and the start of his work night. That hadn't nearly been enough, and he was jonesing for her touch the way a junkie did for drugs.

"So, inventor of the Thinkgasm, tell me all about it."

"Can you put that in the form of a question?"

He raised a brow.

"I guess you didn't watch the *Jeopardy!* clip."

"You were a game-show question? That's some serious fame there, babe."

"Yeah, uh, my bosses didn't appreciate that kind of fame."

"They're idiots."

"They especially didn't appreciate the *Today* show coverage."

"Dicks."

"Well, to be honest, I wasn't crazy about that one, either. They made my work into a big joke—some female guest was trying to Thinkgasm herself on the show. Har, har, let's make fun of women's sexuality and go all *When Harry Met Sally* diner-orgasm-scene on live television."

He reached across the table and took her hand, knowing her well enough to gauge that she was upset. "I'm sorry. I didn't mean to bring up a sore subject. I really was just curious."

She squeezed his hand. "It's okay. I'm the one who's sorry. I guess I'm still a little touchy about it. I mean, it's fine if Lady Gaga tells the world she can think herself off, but let a female psychologist do a major study on it and the sky falls in."

She was right. It *was* unfair, and incredibly sexist. He was a guy, and even he could see it. Fortunately, there were plenty of women in his family—no sisters, but female cousins and aunts, and his very independent mom—who had instilled in Mike, and his brothers, a serious respect for women.

"As for what it is, if you looked it up on Google, I'm sure you already get the basic premise of the Thinkgasm."

"Uh, yeah. Women always were the more imaginative sex. Can you do it?"

"Nope."

"Have you tried?"

"Yep."

He laughed at her disgruntled expression, but it quickly segued into a smile. Her eyes were twinkling now, her good humor returning, so he asked, "Now, be honest, have you tried since you and I have been involved? Because, seriously, I could probably Thinkgasm all over myself just remembering what we did Thursday night."

She licked her lips, obviously remembering, too. There was so much to remember. The sex had been wild. Amazing. He'd done things with her he'd only ever fantasized about doing. While they hadn't tried every one of her naughty toys, they'd definitely put a dent in that box full of sin.

"I'm going to plead the fifth on the grounds that my answer may incriminate me."

Oh, yeah. Some of the things they did would definitely be cause for scandal. They'd pushed limits, tested boundaries, explored just how far they could go. The answer was, pretty far. Lindsey didn't always want to play the submissive game, but whenever they did, she climaxed so many times she was nearly incoherent.

Although Mike would have liked to spend entire nights in her bed and wake up with her every bright, sunny morning, the population of Wild Boar Island made it utterly impossible. Not only was he often on duty overnight, since his was a four-man police department, there was also the fact that his apartment was right over a shop owned by a gossipy busybody. She lived in another apartment across the hall from him, and he'd swear the woman had the hearing of a bat. Since she'd been one of the ones to bring him cakes and pies when he'd first arrived, she was often on the lookout for his return home so she could rush out with something she'd whipped up. When those return-homes occurred late at night, and he wasn't in uniform, she asked intrusive questions about where he'd been.

He and Lindsey had resigned themselves to stolen hours on his evenings off. They were always at her place, and he always left at around four in the morning so he could sneak back home like a kid who'd climbed out the window to go to a kegger. He was dying to stay longer so she could wake up in the morning in his arms. She'd once commented that she'd never actually fallen asleep with a man and was shocked to find she liked it.

He liked it, too. As a matter of fact, he liked everything about her. And as the days had passed, he began to suspect what he was feeling was more than liking.

He just had no idea if she felt the same. Lindsey might have opened up to him a lot—physically and emotionally—but she still kept some mysteries close, and some vulnerabilities closer. She might say she enjoyed falling asleep with him, but she was also the one who always woke him up at 3:00 a.m. and sent him on his way.

He knew she was just protecting him because of his job. Yet, sometimes he caught a haunted look on her face that said spending an entire night with him would require knocking down another of those barriers she kept around herself. And she wasn't quite ready to do it.

"Where did you go?" she murmured.

"Just thinking about you."

"Why do you have to think about me when I'm sitting right across from you?"

He dropped his gaze, looking over the soft, pretty blouse that hid the amazing body to which he was fast becoming addicted. "Lately, I think about you all the time."

She dropped her eyes, staring into her cup and stirring it. "We're not being very discreet."

"Fuck discretion."

A sweet laugh fell from her lips. She quickly quieted, glancing around the café again. "We both know we have to be careful. I can't take any more scandal, and neither can you. Or Callie." As if reminding herself of that, she pulled her hand free of his, fisting it on the table.

"You're sure that's all it is?"

"What do you mean?"

He hadn't intended to bring this up now, and certainly not here. He felt compelled, though, to start trying to batter at those last remaining walls. "I just get the sense there are things you haven't told me."

She didn't pretend to misunderstand, or to hide the truth. "There *are* things I haven't told you."

He waited.

"And I don't intend to."

More bothered by that than he cared to admit, he leaned back in his chair and crossed his arms over his chest. "Care to explain?"

"Look, we're having a great time. A fantastic time," she said, leaning over the table and keeping her voice low. Swallowing visibly, she added, "Let's not make more of it than it is."

Well, shit. That sounded like it should be his line, it was such a guy attitude. He'd always been aware that Lindsey was not a typical woman. She wasn't overly emotional and certainly not clingy. Her independence was attractive, but, to be honest, also a little intimidating.

And if he believed she absolutely meant it, that there was nothing else holding her back, he might take her at her word and write this off as a fling. But he didn't quite believe it. She might not be ready to call it anything more, but that vulnerability in her face, the catch in her voice, revealed that something deep inside her wanted to. He just had to be patient and see if she could ever let herself admit it.

"Okay, I guess you've made things pretty clear."

A frown creased her brow. "Don't you agree?"

"That this is fun but going nowhere?"

She nodded slowly. He looked into her green eyes, seeing uncertainty, as if she wasn't sure exactly what she wanted him to say. He suspected part of her wanted him to agree. That would be the easy way out. Neither of them would have to think about it, or examine it, they could just keep doing what they were doing, and hopefully nobody would get hurt. That was the Lindsay who still hadn't lowered some of those walls, who still needed to control everything, including relationships that could end up hurting her.

Another part, though…well, he wasn't so sure.

"It is what it is," he finally said with a shrug that feigned a disinterest he didn't feel. Such a cop-out of an answer, but it was the best he could do right now.

She glanced away, her mouth tightening. He watched her, reading her reaction, knowing she was feeling a disappointment she hadn't expected to feel. Interesting.

"Very well," she said. "We'll just go on as we have been?"

He didn't push it, as she had to leave for work in a minute. "Sure." Wagging his brows, he added, "We still have half a box to get through. Wasn't that little porpoise thing next?"

She sucked in a shocked breath, not meeting his eye. Color rose in her cheeks.

A blush? From Lindsey? How freakin' adorable.

How on earth the woman could possibly be embarrassed around him he had no idea. It had to be because it was so early in the morning and she didn't have her armor completely in place.

Before either of them could say anything else, the front door opened with a ring of the bell. Lindsey jerked back in her chair. A group of students walked in, and she immediately reached for her purse and stood up. "I've got to go."

He didn't try to argue, understanding. Thinking about

the sex toys one minute and having a bunch of her students walk in the next had to be a little jarring.

"Okay. I'll talk to you later."

She started to walk away, but paused before she'd gone three steps. The teens were at the counter, walking like zombies, not filled with chatter and excitement the way they would be after school. That was probably why Lindsey didn't just walk out. Instead, she dropped a hand on his shoulder and murmured, "I imagine you'll be waiting for me in my bed when I get home at four? With the porpoise?"

He grinned. "Yes, ma'am, I think I will."

She winked at him then walked out, speaking to her students as she exited. They replied easily. No heads came together whispering about who she'd been sitting with. He'd bet they hadn't even noticed.

The kids seemed to like her. Not surprising—she was smart, young and new. He wondered what on earth they'd think if they found out how famous she really was, and he prayed none of her students ever had reason to do a thorough internet search on her.

Intending to go home and sleep for a few hours in preparation for what he hoped would be a hell of a sensual night, Mike got up to leave. Unfortunately, he hadn't even reached the door when someone else came in. Someone who he also prayed never had reason to do research on Lindsey.

"Chief, there you are! I stopped by the station and was told you'd gone off duty and that I might be able to find you here."

He nodded, wondering how early the president of the town council had to get up in the morning to put that much shellac in her hair and that much makeup on her face by 6:30 a.m. "Morning, Mrs. Franklin."

The woman cast a stern, disapproving glance at the

students. They put their heads together, whispering and giggling, and her frown grew so deep her eyes almost disappeared under her brows. "Aren't you supposed to be at school?" she asked querulously.

The teens clutched their coffees and headed for the door. One of them snapped off a salute before exiting, and Mike bit the inside of his cheek to prevent a laugh.

"In my day, children that age wouldn't be allowed to drink coffee," she said, aiming the comment at Alice, the shop owner. "Do you require proof of age before you sell it to them?"

Alice snorted. "I'm not selling cigarettes here, Ida. If you're worried about that, why don't you take a look at the sales of *your* store?"

Flustered, the older woman harrumphed, then leaned in to Mike. "I want an update on the progress you've made on the case."

"Case?" he said, playing dumb, though he knew exactly what she meant. She'd come in to talk to him about that stupid book four times in the past ten days. The fact that she hadn't been able to stir up anybody else into an outraged posse seemed to have made her even more determined to go it alone.

"The pornographer. Ollie informs me you've not assigned a task force to investigate."

A task force? Jesus. The woman watched too many episodes of *Law & Order*. Shaking his head and rubbing his eyes, he explained—again, "Ma'am, there's no pornographer."

"Oh, yes, there is. Someone intentionally left that book on the ground for a child to find it."

Uh-oh, things had gone a step further. Now it wasn't just some sicko who was careless with his things, it was a plot to destroy little minds.

"No, she didn't."

The woman's eyes flared. Her nostrils did, too, as if she'd smelled something juicy. "You said 'she.'"

Calling himself ten kinds of idiot, he snapped, "He *or* she. Mrs. Franklin, as far as I'm concerned, this matter is closed."

"You've discovered who did it, haven't you?"

Making a decision, and hoping he didn't regret it, he said, "Yes, I have. The owner dropped it completely by accident and was horribly embarrassed. I returned the property, and that's the end of the matter."

"Who was it?"

Suddenly appearing more titillated than bossy, Mike had to wonder just how much this twenty-years-a-widow had looked at that book. "That's absolutely none of your business."

She gasped as if he'd slapped her. On the other side of the café, Angie snorted loudly, covering it by coughing into her fist. He'd just done the equivalent of flipping off his boss, but right now, he truly didn't care.

"You can't speak to me like that."

"Ma'am, I'm a police officer. You are a citizen. Even if a crime had been committed—which it hasn't—I wouldn't be at liberty to discuss it with you. Nor would I want to."

"Ollie would have…"

"You didn't hire Ollie, remember?" he asked, suddenly half wishing the council had.

Then he remembered Lindsey, and the fact that he might never have met her if not for this job, and quashed that thought. Even if he didn't stay in this job, the months he'd spent here, under watchful eyes of judgmental people like Mrs. Franklin, would have been worth it, because of Lindsey.

"Now, if you'll excuse me, I'm off duty and I'm going home."

"We're not finished here."

"Yes, Mrs. Franklin, we are. If you have anything else to say to me, you can come by the station tomorrow, because I'm off until late tonight."

And with that, and a nod to Angie, he strode out of the coffee shop, wondering if he'd just effectively ruined his chances of holding on to this job at the end of his probation.

Funny. Somehow, right at this moment, knowing for certain that Lindsey would not be staying here after this school year, he just didn't give a damn.

As SHE FINISHED packing a picnic basket she'd found in the pantry with bread and cheese, grapes and wine, Lindsey asked, "Are you sure this is a good idea?"

Mike cupped her face and brushed his mouth across hers. "It's a beautiful day… We're completely alone. It will be fine."

She hoped so. Because he was right—it was beautiful out. Spring had definitely sprung, and the May days were gorgeously sunny and warm. Even the gardens around her cottage had erupted with daffodils and tulips, the flowers bursting through the weeds and erupting in yellows and reds. The island was truly coming to life. The town was also sprucing up for the tourist season, with more and more shops open on Main Street.

"Come on, this'll probably be our last chance. The tourists will start coming over for weekends in the next week or two. With you working every weekday, we might not have another opportunity."

Oh, he was tempting. As discreet as they tried to be, she did long to just be with him, in the sunshine, holding hands, doing whatever. Well, considering they were bringing along a blanket and heading to an extremely private beach, the "whatever" might be pretty naughty.

"It'll be worth it," he promised. "And it's not like we're going twenty miles away. We're walking through your backyard."

That was true. The small beach on the southernmost tip of the island was accessible through the woods behind her place. According to the locals, only summer people who rented the vacant cottages all around hers went to the beach, so they'd have complete privacy, which made it just about perfect for them.

Seeing Mike naked in the sunlight had become one of her lifelong goals.

Still, she kept an eye peeled as they approached the shoreline and walked down to the small, secluded beach. The sand between the trees and the water was probably only about twenty feet wide, the shoreline curving away into a rocky cliff on one side and into the woods on another. The beach was every bit as private as she'd been led to believe, a little alcove that was probably overcrowded and noisy during the summer, but was as idyllic as a Caribbean lagoon right now.

"It's beautiful. You're *sure* nobody comes down here?" she asked, thinking that if she lived on this island, she'd visit this place as often as she could. It offered such a beautiful contrast—beach and forest—and was tucked away so perfectly by the curves in the landscape, she just couldn't imagine a prettier place on Wild Boar.

He lowered the picnic basket she'd prepared. "I'm sure. I've heard the locals only use the north beach. Besides, it's too cold for swimming still. You won't catch anybody diving into one of the Great Lakes in the middle of May."

"I can't believe it's the middle of May already," she said. "I'd lost track of the days—they're going by so quickly. It really took me by surprise yesterday when one of the kids mentioned Memorial Day coming up. I'm more than halfway through my teaching gig. Less than a month to go."

Time definitely flew when you were having great sex. And she and Mike had been doing a lot of that over the past couple of weeks.

They weren't just having sex, though. Quite often, he'd show up with a bag of groceries and would cook her dinner. Or they'd go for walks in the woods near her cottage. He brought over some tools and fixed the front porch, saying he was afraid she'd step out onto it and crash through the floor.

They even took the ferry across to the mainland one Sunday, pretending not to be together since some other island residents were on board. But once on the other side of the lake, they'd done all the normal things a dating couple did, from going to a movie to having dinner in a pricey restaurant. Seeing Mike in a tailored navy suit had been the highlight of her day, even if they did have to leave early to get the last ferry back so he could be at work by eleven.

She'd spent a lot of time thinking about that day after it ended. She'd found it surprisingly difficult to go back to their sneaking-around type of affair after their day of freedom. But since Mike seemed fine with the status quo, she hadn't said anything about it.

And it seemed especially important after he'd told her about nosy old Mrs. Franklin, who still hadn't given up trying to find out who'd dropped the book in the town parking lot. Realizing that the woman was on the warpath—and that Mike was in her way—Lindsey knew she couldn't put him at any more risk of losing his job. He was on probation; the last thing he needed was for anybody to find out he was dating the "purveyor of pornography."

God, it was so ridiculous. While she was not happy that

a teenage boy had found it, no harm had been done. She was familiar with the Morgan kid—he was eighteen years old, and a senior. He was also the jock of the school, the big man on campus. The girls in her advanced class spoke frankly about how many girls he'd "hooked up" with. If he was still an innocent virgin, then so was Lindsey.

"Hungry?" he asked, interrupting the thoughts she really didn't want to be thinking anyway.

"Starving."

He helped her spread the blanket then they sat together on it. She opened the picnic basket and handed him the bottle of wine and an opener. Removing the crackers and cheese, she said, "Well, it's cheddar and not imported Camembert, but it'll have to do."

"I suppose the grocery store was all out of caviar, too," he said with a grin.

"Afraid so."

"Rats."

"They didn't have those, either," she quipped.

"Ha, ha."

He popped the wine bottle open, pouring them each a glass while she pulled out a container of juicy grapes. She popped one into her mouth, its tartness surprising and refreshing, especially when she chased it with a bit of the white wine.

They sipped silently, both eyeing the gentle waves lapping at the shoreline. If it were even ten degrees warmer, she'd be tempted to dive in, as the water looked so crystalline and beautiful. But the lake had to be frigid; the temperatures still got very cold at night.

"Considering skinny-dipping?" he asked her.

"Not on your life."

"Good. That water's gotta be sixty-five degrees at the most. I doubt my ego could take the shrinkage."

She sipped, eyeing him flirtatiously over the glass. "I *really* don't think you have anything to worry about."

"No?"

"Stop fishing for compliments."

"Yes, teacher."

Popping another grape into her mouth, she bit into it. Mike caught her by surprise when he leaned over and covered her lips with his. He immediately slid his tongue against hers, stealing the grape right out of her mouth.

"Hey, that was mine."

"I'll get you another one."

It was his turn to bite into a firm grape, and Lindsey's turn to steal some of it right out of his mouth. They'd played so many sexy games, but never yet with food. She liked the way the stolen grape tasted, loved the unique flavor Mike brought to something already so sweet and juicy.

Lifting her hand and cupping his jaw, she angled her head and deepened the kiss. Their tongues tangled and danced, pushing and pulling. He explored her entire mouth, like he couldn't get enough of her, and she was soon breathless. Kissing Mike had become as essential as breathing.

"I've dreamed about making love to you out in the open," he said.

"That's probably because we've been keeping this whole thing secret."

"Is that your professional opinion, Dr. Smith?"

"No. It's just that I feel the same way."

She was falling for Mike, in a big way. His body had become the most important place on earth, his kisses a daily requirement. If a day went by when she didn't see him, she felt empty and miserable. And if she went more than two without making love with him, she became restless and needy, attacking him the next time they were alone. Lindsey didn't know if it was love, never having been in love before. She only knew her whole world came alive when she was with him.

His warm hands slid down her body, pulling her top free of the waistband of her jeans. She quivered when those strong fingers brushed against her skin as he pulled the shirt up and off. He looked down at her breasts, covered in a lacy pink bra, his expression both admiring and hungry.

She had grown addicted to being looked at like that. As if, in his eyes, she was the most beautiful, desirable woman alive.

"I can't get enough of you," he admitted, bending to press a hot, openmouthed kiss to her nape.

"You're welcome to keep trying," she said, already growing limp and boneless as he kissed his way down her throat.

He licked the hollow then scraped his teeth over her collarbone. When he reached her bra strap, he nudged it off, reaching around behind her to unfasten it. Lindsey helped, letting the thing fall off her body.

The moment her breasts were uncovered, Mike bent to lick one, kissing the tip, sucking her nipple delicately. She sighed, loving the tenderness of it. He was almost worshipful, and acted as though he had all the time in the world to give them both all sorts of pleasure.

"Let me see all of you," he said. "Please."

She nodded, unfastening her jeans and letting him help her pull them down. Kicking off her sandals, she caught her panties with the tip of her finger and began tugging them down, as well.

He stopped her. "Let me."

She smiled, enjoying this slow, deliberate side of him. She'd seen him in so many moods; they'd made love in all sorts of ways. But this was something new. She felt like a sun goddess being worshipped.

Lying back on the blanket, she lifted a little so he could slide her panties off. He took his time, scraping his hands along the length of her legs. Once she was completely naked, he knelt beside her and gazed down at her, his expression the picture of desire.

"Haven't you looked at me enough?"

"Not in the daylight. I'm imprinting this on my memory."

His attention was flattering, and arousing. Savoring the heat of the warmth on her bare skin, Lindsey stretched and purred like a cat, lying lazily in a sunbeam. She felt almost elemental, protected in this cove. A light wind blew through the woods, sending dry leaves tumbling. The lap of the waves created a slow, steady melody. She was aware of every sensation, from the softness of the blanket beneath her skin to the smell of the wine they'd sipped.

Mike said nothing; he simply began to strip out of his clothes. Slowly. She watched his every move, her breath catching as that amazing body was revealed in all its glory.

He was so incredibly defined—arms rippling with muscle, shoulders so broad, chest so powerful. Unable to resist, she reached up and brushed her fingertips through the wiry hair between his nipples, following the trail down his stomach. She scraped her nails over his amazing abs, delighting in the flexing of muscle beneath that perfect golden skin.

He stood up to finish undressing. She stayed there beneath him, looking up at him as if she'd been laid out as a banquet. His eyes never left her, and she stretched and curved, basking in the sunlight, getting hotter by the second. When his pants dropped, she swallowed hard. When his shorts followed, she hissed, shocked, as always, by the potent beauty of his sex. It was huge, intimidating and powerful. And she wanted it desperately.

"I've grown quite fond of that," she admitted.

He knelt beside her. "What, this?" he asked, taking her hand and putting it on his cock.

Moisture raced to her sex and she bit her lip. Encircling him as much as she could, she slid her hand up and down… Slow, easy strokes. Mike watched her intently for a few long moments, then, when it got too much, he closed his eyes and dropped his head back, savoring her attention.

There was such power in this act. She literally held his maleness in her hand and could, if she kept going, bring him to a rollicking climax. While part of her wanted to, another part screamed, *No way.*

She wanted him inside her. Wanted that heat, that strength, that hardness. She wanted him to split her open and fill her up and bury himself so deep she would never again feel empty because he would have made himself a part of her.

"Make love to me, Mike," she whispered, dying for him.

He reached for his pants pocket. She stilled his hand. "You don't have to do that."

He raised a curious brow.

"I called my doctor's office in Chicago the Monday after we first had sex and had her call in a birth control pill prescription. I've been on them long enough for it to be safe."

His dark eyes gleamed with pleasure. She suspected he'd wanted to take her with absolutely no barrier as much as she'd wanted to be taken that way.

"Did you have to wear a bag over your head when you got the prescription filled at the local pharmacy?"

She laughed softly. "No, but I did mention to the lady at the counter that I really hoped they'd even out my horrible, irregular periods."

His turn to laugh. Then the laughter faded, and they

were once again focused on every touch, every quiver, every sigh. They exchanged long, slow kisses and longer, intimate touches. He seemed content to touch every inch of her, giving her toes as much attention as he did her breasts. And in the sunlight, she was free to explore all the wonderful ridges and planes of his body.

Finally, when the sweet tension was almost unbearable, he moved between her thighs. She savored the weight of him on top of her; the hair on his legs brushed against the smoothness of hers, his flat nipples rubbed her taut, sensitized ones.

He kissed her deeply, erotically, as he slid his cock against her slickness. She parted her legs farther, arching up to welcome him. Then she wrapped her arms around his neck, clinging to him as they shared kiss after deep, wet kiss.

He entered her slowly, sinking into her a little at a time, and she moaned against his lips. The heat of him, the strength of him, filled her mind as well as her body and she found herself focusing on every tiny sensation. Her skin was entirely sensitized, from her head to her toes. She had never been as utterly in tune with herself as she was now, which made it all the more easy to focus on the intense sensations Mike provided.

"This is amazing," she whispered, kissing his earlobe, scraping her nails on his back.

"Yeah, it is. You're so hot, Lindsey, so sweet and wet and tight."

The lack of a condom had taken things from amazing to heart-stopping. Having nothing separating them, not even the barest sliver of rubber, made more of a difference than she'd ever have imagined. When he finally thrust deep, filling her completely, she screamed out the bliss of it to the blue sky above. A startled bird took wing from a nearby tree, cawing as it streaked across the sky, and for a moment, she knew how it felt to fly.

It would be like this. This weightlessness, buoyed by the cloud of tenderness and emotion surging between her and Mike. And he was taking her high, so incredibly high.

They found a rhythm and began to rock to it, thrusting easily, slowly. Then faster. And faster.

She was soon gasping, clinging to him with hungry desperation. He'd taken her high enough. Now it was time to soar and fall back to earth.

"Please," she begged. "Please, Mike."

He braced himself on one elbow, moving his other hand between their hot, slick bodies. The very moment he scraped his fingers across her clit, her climax erupted, low and strong, building and shooting out until she felt it to the very ends of her hair.

"Oh, yes!" she yelled, not giving a damn if she scared every bird or boar off the island.

Mike groaned and thrust, his breaths harsh, his eyes glazing. Staring at him, thinking about what he'd just given her—what he was still giving her—was enough to push her to the edge again. When he finally spilled over into his own ecstasy, she followed him, spinning, flying, falling.

But convinced he'd be there to catch her.

Afterward, spent, they collapsed together on the blanket, limbs entwined, heart rates slowing. He still held her close, kissing her temple, stroking her belly. Lindsey went from closing her eyes and dozing off to staring straight up to enjoy the beautiful blue sky overhead.

"This is wonderful," she whispered. "I can't remember a better day. My very first picnic."

"Seriously?"

"Yes. I always wanted to go on one."

"Your family…"

She stiffened, unable to stop the reflexive reaction.

"I'm sorry. None of my business."

Not speaking for a moment, she considered what to say. She and Mike had gotten close, in just about every way. But there was that one part of her life she'd never told him about. Never come close to telling him about.

She wasn't sure she was ready to share the whole thing, but she could at least try to do what she knew he wanted her to do: open up to him, knock down those last walls she kept wrapped so protectively around her heart.

"I didn't have the big-family, happy childhood you had," she finally said. Clearing her throat, she added, "I was an only child."

"Hey, only child—more presents at Christmas."

If her laugh was bitter, she supposed she could be forgiven. "There were rarely Christmases. No birthdays. My parents were big believers in the what-doesn't-kill-you-makes-you-stronger philosophy."

"You were abused?" he asked, the words stark and pained.

"I never really thought of it that way. I mean, certainly not sexually, and physically it didn't usually go beyond an occasional spanking."

She heard him let out a long, slow breath, and realized he'd been holding it, waiting for her to answer his question. Realizing he'd been worried about something that might have happened to her long, long ago, she could feel another rush of emotion toward this man filling her heart.

"What haven't you said yet?" he asked.

"Well, I suppose Children and Families considered me abused. They took me away and I went into foster care for a couple of months after I was found wandering through the projects where we lived one night. I'd woken up alone and gone looking for my parents, who were at a bar. I was seven."

His muscles tightened; she could feel it from his shoulder down to his legs. His reaction didn't surprise her—this wasn't easy for her to talk about, and it wouldn't be easy for somebody like Mike, who only wanted to protect people, to hear.

"Jesus."

"It's okay. It's over. They were a little better, for a while, anyway, after they got me back. Eventually I was old enough to take care of myself and it didn't matter anymore. They're both long gone. As is the little lost girl I was."

"But you're alone."

"I've got Callie," she insisted. *And you.* But she didn't quite dare to say that aloud. "She and her family pretty much took me in during high school and gave me the closest thing to a normal life I've ever had. That's why she's like my sister. There's nothing I wouldn't do for her."

"I'm glad she was there for you. But I'm still so sorry, angel."

"I had it worse than some, but not as bad as others. And in the end, I succeeded beyond their wildest expectations, and my own dreams. I refused to let whatever shitty things might have happened in my past determine my future."

He kissed her cheek, gently stroking her hip, tracing little circles on her skin. "You're an amazing woman, Lindsey Smith. Thank you for telling me."

She turned to look at him, cupping his face, seeing the moisture in his eyes from the tears he wanted to shed for her. Her heart twisted, something broke open, and she found herself actually shedding a tear, too.

"You're an amazing man, Mike. Thank you so much for making me trust you enough to tell you."

9

WHEN MIKE HEARD a knock on the door of his apartment on the Saturday of Memorial Day weekend, he figured his landlady was bringing him some flag-shape cookies, or maybe a red, white and blue cake. He considered ignoring the knock, since he'd just gotten out of the shower and wore only a pair of jeans, but the landlady would just use her key to let herself into his place and "surprise" him.

She'd done that once—*surprising* him. He'd been surprised all right, considering he'd been walking naked from his bedroom to the kitchen to put on some coffee.

He'd hoped that would have taught her a lesson. Instead, if anything, he suspected she'd be quicker to use her key now than she'd been before that embarrassing incident.

"Just a second," he said, tossing the towel he'd used on his hair down. He made sure it landed on top of the large package he'd received in yesterday's mail. He somehow didn't think his landlady would react well to seeing a big foam device called a Sex Wedge standing in his apartment.

Lindsey might have all the small toys covered, but he'd spotted this thing online when he'd been looking up her name on Google—gotta love targeted advertising—and had decided to buy it. All those other items had been samples. This was a present only for her. To be used only with him. He could hardly wait.

For a second, he wondered if it might be Lindsey at the door, that she'd found some excuse to stop by. She'd never been to his place, since it was right in the middle of town with absolutely zero privacy. But maybe she'd dreamed up a reason.

Ever hopeful, he pulled the door open but was shocked to see four people standing on his doorstep.

"Surprise!" they all said.

"Oh, my God, Nick? Iz?" He turned to the other couple. "Mark and Noelle? What the hell are you all doing here?"

His cousin Nick's bombshell wife, Izzie, pushed past him into the living room. "Are you going to invite us in?"

"You're in," he said with a laugh, pressing a quick kiss onto her cheek. His spirits were rising by the second. He grabbed Mark and hugged him hard. "How are you doing, man?"

"Surviving."

Nick clapped him on the back. "I'm okay, too, if it matters."

"Last time I checked, you were running a strip club and surrounded by women who are almost as beautiful as your wife. I *know* what kind of people surround Mark in his job, and they aren't beautiful women." And he had the scars to prove it.

"Yeah, I'm familiar with the scum he has to deal with, too," said Noelle, Mark's wife, offering her husband a pointed stare. She was just as pretty as Izzie, in a softer, quieter way. Also a brunette, Noelle looked every inch a thirty-ish wife and mother.

Izzie and Nick didn't have kids yet, and he wasn't sure they ever would. They were definitely the edgiest couple of the family, with her stripping background and his hard-ass, ex-Marine demeanor. But anyone could look at them and see they were still totally crazy in love. They didn't need kids to complete their family; they just needed each other.

Speaking of which, Mike peered out into the hall, then glanced back toward Mark, who was every inch a proud papa. "Where are the rugrats?"

"Mama's got them," Mark explained. "It's a big third-generation sleepover at the grandparents' tonight."

"Is everyone there?" he asked, wondering how on earth they'd all fit into his Aunt Rosa and Uncle Anthony's house.

"Most of 'em. Joe and Meg dropped the girls off, and Tony and Gloria's two youngest are there, as well."

All that was left were Lottie's daughter and Luke's twins and the whole gang would be represented. There were other cousins, children of his dad's youngest two brothers, who had college-age kids. They hadn't even started marrying and settling down. But he had no doubt they would—it was the Santori way. By the time all the branches on the family tree reproduced, they could probably populate a small town.

"Get this," Mark said. "Tony's oldest isn't there 'cause he's on a date. Can you frigging believe that? Kid's not even thirteen years old and already has girlfriends."

It sounded like little Anthony was a chip off the old block.

Nick elbowed his twin, who was a little shorter and a little broader. They were fraternal, not identical, though they'd never be mistaken for anything but brothers. "I seem to recall you doing a little girlfriend juggling yourself in middle school."

Izzie smirked. "Pot, have you met Kettle here?"

They all laughed, and Mike thought about the family gathering going on back in Chicago. He wondered if he and his brothers might be doing the same thing with their own kids in another five years or so. And not for the first time, he experienced a twist of loneliness in his gut and wondered if he'd made a huge mistake by moving here, so far away from everyone he knew and cared about.

Except Lindsey.

Yeah. She was here. And frankly, considering he had fallen crazy in love with her, she was enough.

"I don't have a lot of room in this place, but feel free to sit wherever there's a spot," he said, gesturing toward the couch. He went into the kitchen and grabbed the two chairs that fronted his small butcher-block table, and carried them in, as well. "Do you want coffee? Anything?"

"I'd kill for a Diet Coke," said Izzie.

"Sorry, I don't have any. I could run down to the general store and get some."

Noelle's eyes rounded. "General store? Good grief, Mike, you said this was a small town, but I didn't realize you'd moved to Walton's Mountain."

He shrugged. "Yeah, it takes a little getting used to."

He didn't dare mention the Irish pizza place. As the sons of the man who owned one of the best Italian restaurants in Chicago, Nick and Mark might feel honor-bound to go over there and raise a little hell.

Getting his cousins' wives some coffee, and Nick and Mark each a beer, he excused himself to go into the bedroom and call Lindsey. She'd been expecting him to come down by two, and it was now after that.

Since he wasn't sure how long his family members would stay, he couldn't tell her what time he'd make it down. He heard the disappointment in her voice, but knew better than to suggest she come up and make it a six-some. Even after all these weeks, she still seemed content to sneak around and keep their relationship strictly between them.

He wasn't going to be content with that much longer.

They were coming close to D-day…aka, the last day of school. After that, there would be no reason for Lindsey to remain on Wild Boar. Her friend would have the whole summer with her baby, and Lindsey could go back to Chicago and find out where she stood with her job and all the rest of it.

Mike honestly had no idea where he fit into her life, but oh, God, did he hope she wanted him somewhere in it. She hadn't said it… They still danced around the subject of their relationship being anything other than a sexy affair. But he caught her looking at him sometimes, when they were making love, or just holding hands watching a movie, and he believed she cared for him. She just hadn't been able to lower those walls enough to admit it yet.

"I'll call you as soon as I figure out what's going on and how long they're staying, okay? I doubt it'll be overnight—the inn's booked solid for the holiday weekend."

"Okay. Have fun with your family. I know you've missed them."

"Actually, right now, you're the one I miss."

"You saw me yesterday."

"Yeah, for breakfast. It's been over twenty-four hours."

"Better watch out there, buddy, or somebody will think you're smitten."

"If that means they'll think I'm crazy about you, they'd be right."

She didn't respond, but he heard a sweet little sigh, and suspected she was pleased by the comment.

Hey, maybe they were getting somewhere.

Ending the call, he walked out of his bedroom to rejoin the others in his living room. To his surprise, they were not sitting on the couches and chairs where he'd left them. In fact, they were all standing in a semicircle, staring down at something on the floor between them. As soon as he entered, four heads jerked up, four sets of eyes staring at him assessingly.

"What's going on?"

"I dunno, Mike. Why don't you tell us?" asked Izzie in her naughtiest voice.

Not getting it, he walked around the back of the couch so he could see what they'd all been gaping at.

"Oh, hell."

It was the sex wedge. Big, graphic, with bold lettering and a superhot illustration of its versatile uses, the thing would draw anybody's eye. Considering it was here in his bachelor apartment, and none of his family were aware he'd been dating anyone, it must have been much too interesting to escape notice.

"So?" Noelle asked. "Who is she?"

"Who's who?"

"Oh, puh-lease," Izzie said. She pointed to the box again. "If you were lonely and single, this package would contain a blow-up doll. Obviously this is not something you use unless you've got somebody to use it with."

Mike swiped a hand through his hair, embarrassed as hell. What was it with the women in his family that they always got into everybody else's business?

Nick and Mark exchanged a look and chuckled, obviously having noticed his discomfiture. "You might as well confess," Mark said. "They're going to nag you until you do."

"Where'd you meet her? Does she live here?" Izzie peered around her husband's shoulder toward the bedroom. "Is she hiding in there?"

"Of course not," Mike snapped. Throwing himself onto

the couch, he admitted, "Her name's Lindsey. I met her on the ferry, and that's as much as you need to know."

Nick cleared his throat.

"Yes?" Mike asked.

"Can I ask just one more thing?"

"What is it?"

"Where'd you get that thing? Because, damn, dude, I want one."

Izzie did that knuckle-punching thing wives did to their husbands. Nick grinned and rubbed his arm, then threw it over her shoulders and drew her close.

"That's not appropriate," she said, sounding all prim.

"Sorry. Everybody knows how appropriate you are."

She narrowed her eyes and stuck her index finger in his chest. "Shut up, Nick Santori, or I'll never make you my special cannoli again."

His superconfident cousin dropped to one knee and clutched at his chest as if wounded. "Don't ever say that to me again! I'll do anything you say."

"Ass," she mumbled, swiping her hand through his hair and bending down to press a kiss on his mouth.

Mark and Noelle had returned to the couch, sitting close, their hands entwined. They were watching Nick and Izzie, almost like parents watching misbehaving kids, which was pretty funny since they were all the same age. But he supposed that pretty well summed up the relationships. Nick and Izzie were playful and wicked. Mark and Noelle were tender and sweet. And all four of them were happier than Mike had ever expected to be in his entire life.

But maybe he'd been wrong about that.

"So, where's Lindsey? Let's get her and all go have lunch. I want to try one of these quaint little diners," Noelle said.

He was shaking his head before she'd finished. "She won't."

"Why not?"

"It's complicated."

"Are we not good enough to meet your girlfriend?" Nick asked, just to give him grief.

"That's not it. It's just that there's no privacy on the island, and we're trying to avoid everyone talking about what's going on between us."

"Uh, then, cuz, you might want to close up that box and tape it shut," said Mark.

"I wasn't expecting company."

"Were you gonna walk down the street with it on your shoulder to take to her place?"

"Point taken. I'd better buy some tape when I'm out."

For now, though, he just decided to enjoy hanging out with his family. Other than spending it with Lindsey, he couldn't think of a better way to spend the day.

They sat down again, catching up. Mike got all the news from home, enjoying hearing about his own brother, Leo, and his very pregnant wife. Hopefully he'd get back to Chicago to see them soon, before the baby came. Hell, by the time the baby was born, he might be out of a job and living who knew where.

A month ago, that might have really bothered him. Now, though…not so much. It wasn't just the realization that Lindsey wasn't going to be on the island much longer. He also wasn't sure he wanted to be here, either, with or without her. This nonsense with Mrs. Franklin and the daily battles with Ollie were bad enough. There was also the whole atmosphere of having to sneak around and guard every moment of his privacy because somebody always wanted to violate it.

He'd come to Wild Boar Island searching for a certain

kind of life. Now that he had it, he wasn't sure he wanted it anymore.

"So, Mike, tell us the truth. Are you really happy living here?" asked Mark.

Mike opened his mouth, about to assure his family he was just fine. He couldn't lie to them, though. "No, not really. I kinda hate it."

"Oh, honey," said Noelle, patting his hand, as if he were a kid who'd gotten his lunch money stolen.

He laughed softly. "That was an exaggeration. It's not that bad. The people are nice." He again thought about Mrs. Franklin, who was still carping about that damn book. "For the most part."

"You're not in love with your job then?" asked Nick.

"No, can't say that I am." He suddenly remembered what Leo had told him last month—about his cousins having some kind of business opportunity to discuss. "What did you have in mind?"

Nick and Mark exchanged a look, each of them smiling. Then they leaned forward and began to explain.

And with every word they said, Mike began to envision a completely different future than he'd ever imagined. In fact, a whole new world of possibilities opened up before his eyes.

He just wondered what it might mean for him and Lindsey, or if she'd ever want more than an affair with him.

AFTER MIKE'S CALL, Lindsey waited around the cottage for a while, wondering what to do. Their plans for the day had included another picnic. Because the summer tourists were flooding the island, that picnic was going to be on her living room floor, but still, she had been looking forward to it. Hopefully, it wouldn't be canceled altogether and they'd at least get to have it tomorrow or Monday. Mike was working nights all weekend, but she definitely planned to fill up his days. At least, as soon as he showed up.

But the hours ticked by and he *didn't* show up. When she glanced at the clock and saw it was after four, she realized the picnic plans would definitely have to be put off for another day.

She also realized she was hungry. She'd shopped for their special, romantic meal and hadn't bought much in the way of groceries. Having no real food in the house, she decided to head into town and grab a bite to eat at one of the diners.

Not having heard from Mike, and assuming he was hanging out with his family, she didn't want to go to the diner on Main Street. That was too close to his place and if she happened to end up at the same restaurant, it might seem too much like she was spying. Or merely desperate.

When she pulled into the parking lot of the diner just south of town a half hour later, she realized it was a good thing she'd come so early. She had heard stories about how the summer tourists filled every corner of the island from Memorial Day through Labor Day. Now she had proof. The roads were busy, the parking lots full. Tourists streamed into and out of the shops and several groups were awaiting tables in the diner.

Deciding to just order something to go, she walked up to the counter. But before she even caught a waitress's attention, she heard her name.

"Lindsey!"

Glancing over her shoulder, she saw Mike waving from across the crowded eatery. He sat with two *extremely* good-looking, dark-haired men, and two very pretty brunettes.

Mike got up and came over to her, maneuvering his way through the crowd. She noted how relaxed and happy he looked. Having his family visit had done him a lot of good.

If she'd had any family she wanted to claim, she supposed she would feel the same way.

"Hi," she said when he reached her.

"Hi. I tried to call you at the cottage a few minutes ago."

"Oh?"

"Yeah. My cousins and their wives have been harassing me and calling me the worst guy in the world for not inviting you to join us for dinner. They're heading back on the seven o'clock ferry and really wanted to meet you." He leaned closer, lowering his voice. "I couldn't really explain…"

That they were secret lovers? That this was supposed to be a short-term fling, and she and Mike might not see each other again once she left the island in another week?

Oh, God, the very thought of that stabbed her in the heart. She was shocked to find moisture in her eyes, and blinked rapidly to keep him from noticing it.

What was happening to her? If just the idea of losing Mike was enough to make her tear up—yes, she, Lindsey, who never cried—what on earth was going to happen when she actually had to leave here? When reality came knocking and she stopped having the luxury of a secret affair with the man of her dreams, and instead had to return to her competitive job and her high-stress life. How would she possibly survive? Most of all, how would she survive *without him?*

"Hey, are you okay?" He took her arm, obviously concerned. "What's wrong?"

"Nothing," she insisted, not wanting to reveal how fragile she was feeling. "I'm fine."

Across the restaurant, she noticed four faces watching them avidly. Their heads came together to whisper, and they all offered her welcoming smiles and gestures. It appeared they really did want her to join them.

And suddenly, she wanted to. She was so tired of sneaking around, never being able to risk a smile at him for fear it would be correctly interpreted. Never able to show that she and Mike had more than a passing acquaintance, though she knew him more intimately than she'd ever known anyone in her life. She was sick of all of it.

"Yes, Mike, I'd love to join you," she said, making her decision. Then, just as quickly, she backpedaled a little. "I mean, as long as it's okay with you."

"Are you kidding?" he asked, giving her a disbelieving look. "I'd love it. And for what it's worth, nearly all the people in this restaurant are outsiders. Other than the waitresses, I don't recognize any locals."

Oh. So he *was* still worried about that.

She sighed inwardly, knowing it wasn't fair to be bothered by it. Mike was just playing by the rules she, herself, had laid down. Perhaps as the end of his six-month probationary period drew closer, he was becoming more concerned about keeping his job. He wouldn't want any kind of scandal or gossip to interfere with that, especially since he'd already made an enemy of Mrs. Franklin over her book.

"Come on, we have an extra chair already."

With his hand on the small of her back, he led her through the crowded place. Lindsey's steps slowed the closer they got.

The whole family thing had sounded fine a minute ago. Now, though, she had begun to feel like an inmate walking toward an execution.

This was so far out of her realm of experience. She had never once been introduced to the family of someone she was dating. And of course she'd never introduced hers to anyone.

The closest she'd come to having a family was when

she'd been with Callie and her parents. Even then, she'd always been aware that she was an outsider. She'd never quite fit in. This close-knit Italian clan would take one look at her and realize she was not the right woman for Mike—not warm enough, not nice enough, not loving enough. *Wrong, wrong, wrong.*

"Linds?" he asked, as if sensing her tension. He leaned close to whisper, "It'll be fine. They're obnoxious but they're also pretty great."

Licking her lips and nodding, she let him pull out her chair then sat down. Mike introduced her to his cousins and their wives, and all four of them immediately tried to make her comfortable, just chatting and including her in their conversations. She listened quietly for a little while, though she waited for them to make her the full focus of their attention.

It didn't take long.

"So, Lindsey, Mike says you met on the ferry?" said Noelle, Mark's wife, who'd said she worked for a children's charity organization in Chicago.

"Yes, on the day I first moved to the island." She blew out a hard breath. "It was absolutely miserable, and he pretty much stopped me from leaping overboard."

"I *know,* right?" said Izzie, who had one of those big, sexy personalities that drew the eyes of everyone in the room. Her formfitting shirt and tight cropped pants emphasized a va-va-voom figure, but she seemed so down to earth that Lindsey couldn't help but like her. "I thought I was going to be sick all the way over."

"And it's beautiful out," Mike interjected. "You should have come over on a stormy day in April."

"Thanks but no thanks," his cousin's wife said.

Noelle's turn to ask the next question. "And you're substitute teaching for your friend, whose baby is in the hospital?"

Lindsey cast a quick glance at Mike. Obviously he'd been talking about her to his family. A lot.

He shrugged sheepishly, a sexy grin on his face. Oh, lord, a woman could forgive the man anything when he gave her that smile.

"Yes, I am."

"How's the baby doing?"

"Beautifully," she said, probably sounding as relieved as she felt after each conversation she had with Callie. "The doctors say they're going to let him come home next week. Callie and her husband are beyond thrilled."

And she was thrilled for them. She had gotten together with Billy last week, and realized why Callie was so crazy about him. It was quite obvious that he adored Callie, and that made him good enough in Lindsey's book.

She'd also taken the ferry over to visit Callie, Billy and the baby at the hospital. The young couple was stressed to the limits of any parents' endurance, but they were still so hopeful for the future and so trusting that their son would be all right. Whenever she thought about her life, and the choices she'd made, she was reminded that she would never regret this small sacrifice that helped set her friends' minds at ease.

Of course, how could she ever regret it when it had brought Mike into her world?

"What I want to know," Nick said with a half smirk, "is how on earth did this ugly SOB ever talk you into going out with him?"

Her back stiffened. The others laughed, and she realized this good-natured joshing was all routine to them. Mike rolled his eyes, taking no offense. It was all just part of the family dynamic.

"Actually, it sort of started when he came to my door in an official capacity." Pasting an innocent expression on her face, she glanced at Mike. "Remember?"

"Oh, yeah," he told her, those brown eyes twinkling. "Lindsey dropped something in the municipal parking lot and caused quite a stir when a teenager found it."

"What did you drop?" asked Izzie, looking titillated. "It wasn't your underwear, was it?"

She laughed out loud. "Of course not. How would I drop my underwear in a public parking lot?"

"My wife is capable of dropping her underwear in many places."

Izzie reached across the table and punched Nick in the shoulder. He grinned, apparently well used to it.

"It was just a book."

Mike looked around the crowded diner, which was so loud it was hard to hear the person next to you, much less somebody at the next table. Still, to be safe, he leaned in and lowered his voice. "A very steamy book."

"I love romance novels," said Noelle with a happy sigh.

"Not that kind," Lindsey said. Heat rose in her face and she wished she'd never started this conversation. "It was, uh, a copy of the *Kama Sutra,*" she admitted.

Izzie squealed, Nick and Mark both burst into laughter and Noelle giggled into her hand. Lindsey laughed with them, finding herself liking this quartet a lot. She wondered if Mike's brothers were similar to Nick and Mark, and suspected they were.

"Now, give me some dirt," she said. "What was Mike like as a little boy."

"A pain in the ass," said Nick with a shrug.

"Nah," said Mark, "he was cute. Rafe was closer to our age, but we usually let Leo and Mikey tag along on our escapades."

"Leo's the middle brother?"

"Yeah," said Mike.

"Leonardo," said Nick. He crossed his arms, gave his cousin a sly look and added, "Raphael's the oldest, and Michelangelo here is the baby."

The waitress had just brought Lindsey a glass of water, and she'd been about to put it to her mouth. But she slowly lowered it, staring at Nick, then at Mike.

He just groaned, glaring at his older cousin.

"Are you serious? Your name is Michelangelo?"

A heavy sigh, then he admitted, "Yeah."

"And your brothers are Leonardo and Raphael?"

She was about to ask if his family had a big thing for art when Nick spoke again. "Didn't he ever mention that his parents had an obsession with the Teenage Mutant Ninja Turtles?"

"How many times do I have to threaten your life before you stop telling people that?" asked Mike through a pasted-on smile.

Lindsey, who vaguely remembered the cartoon characters, had been trying to puzzle out the dates when she realized Nick was again yanking Mike's chain. Feeling stupid, she slapped herself on the forehead. She was often accused of taking things too literally. *Maybe well justified.*

"Behave, boys, or we'll tattle to your moms," said Izzie.

"What will you do once you've finished the substitute teaching job, Lindsey?" asked Mark, who resembled Mike more than his twin did. Though they both had the big, solid build, incredibly broad shoulders and powerful chests.

"I'm not sure. I'm playing that by ear," she said.

That was true. She had talked to one of the partners at the clinic last week, and he'd admitted that they really missed her. But since he'd also admitted that the senior partner was still very unhappy about that whole *Today* show thing, it may not have been long enough for them to welcome her back.

"But you'll be returning to Chicago, right?" asked Izzie, who was exchanging knowing glances with her husband.

"I'm certain I will."

"Oh, how nice. Too bad Mike doesn't live there anymore," said Izzie. "He just can't stand the city, now that he's all about small-town life and white picket fences. He's found heaven, I guess."

"White picket fences?" she asked, totally confused.

Mike was shaking his head, muttering under his breath about his pushy family.

"Is there something going on?" Lindsey asked.

"Yeah, my cousins are using *your* tricks and pulling some reverse psychology on me," he said.

"Your tricks?" Nick asked, suddenly very alert. "What's that mean?"

Mike sent her an apologetic wince, and she realized he hadn't meant to reveal that bit of personal information. Sensing that being secretive would make it an even bigger deal, she shrugged it off and tried to sound blasé. "I'm not a teacher, really, I'm a psychologist."

"Yeah, that's Dr. Smith to you," Mike said, dropping a hand on her shoulder as if showing the others he was proud of her.

It was a sweet gesture. Kinda nice and protective. Then again, that was Mike. Superprotective. She just wondered if he had any protective instincts when it came to his own well-being. If he did, he probably wouldn't have gotten involved with a woman who was a tabloid scandal. Oh, and one who wasn't even sure she was capable of letting anyone close enough to maintain a long-term relationship.

"Oh, my God!" Noelle said, her voice raised in surprise. Her mouth fell open as she stared at Lindsey. Her eyes had grown huge in her face, and she appeared stunned. "It's *you*. You're *the* Dr. Lindsey Smith!"

Lindsey grimaced, trying to shrink down in her seat.

"Shh," Mike hissed. "That's not common knowledge around here."

Blanching, his cousin-in-law immediately stammered her apologizes. "I'm so sorry. It's just, I was trying to figure out why you looked familiar to me. I didn't put it together until he mentioned you were a doctor."

"All right, what's going on?" asked Izzie. "What are we missing? Who is she?"

Noelle leaned closer to her sister-in-law and whispered, "The Thinkgasm."

Across the table, Mark and Nick both perked up, glancing at each other and then back at their wives. Lindsey wanted to sink into the floor since Noelle's wording had made it sound as if she, Lindsey, *was* something called a Thinkgasm. God, could this get any worse?

Izzie shrugged. "That sex fad? What about it?"

"She invented it."

Rubbing her forehead, Lindsey sighed and said, "I didn't invent it. I just studied it."

"I mean, she's the one who did the study that made it so popular in the news lately."

Izzie smiled in visible delight. "That is *so* boss! Can you show me how to do it?"

"What is this Thinkgasm, Dr. Smith?" Nick asked.

"Remember when I dragged you to that dinner-theater production of *The Music Man?*" Noelle asked her husband. "Where the guy tells the kids they need to learn via the think method. If they think they can play music, they will. It's similar to that."

"I'm pretty sure I was asleep by that point in the musical," Mark said, earning a glare. "Sorry, *Doctor* Smith."

"Okay, subject change, right now," Mike said, his tone brooking no argument. "This is not the time or the place."

The others fell silent. She could have kissed him right there in the middle of the diner. He'd taken charge and immediately set out to protect her, as always. What on earth she'd ever done right in her life to deserve meeting him, she honestly had no idea.

She was about to open her mouth to thank him, but before she could do it, she heard a male voice from behind her. And the words died in her mouth.

"Doctor, huh? I knew there was somethin' funny about you."

She jerked around and looked up to see Mike's deputy, the obnoxious Ollie Dickinson, standing right behind her chair. He wore a self-satisfied smirk, one that had been on his face every single time she'd laid eyes on the man.

Dear God, how much did he overhear?

Reminding herself not to panic, she forced herself to offer the obnoxious man a polite nod. How much damage could he do, even if he had heard anything? The school year was almost over—she only had four more days after Monday's holiday. Then she'd be out of here, no longer around to be hurt by any gossip he chose to impart.

Of course, Mike and Callie would both still be.

Damn it.

Mike pushed his chair back and slowly rose to his feet. "Officer Dickinson. Is there a problem?"

Mike's body was tight and hard, from stiff shoulders down to his clenched hands. Tension rolled off him, and she hoped he was able to keep his cool.

"No problem, Chief," the other officer said, lazy and insolent. "I was just stopping by to get something to eat and noticed you and *Doctor* Smith sitting together all nice and cozy. Figured I'd come over and say hey."

"I'm having dinner with my family," Mike said.

The man looked around. As if realizing their cousin was facing a foe, Mark and Nick both slowly rose to their feet, too.

Good lord, what a sight. Lindsey held her breath, realizing the entire diner was falling quiet. Conversations halted, forks stopped tinkling, dishes weren't being plunked down. Everyone in the place was watching the scene unfolding at their table. She couldn't say whether that was because they could all sense the drama, or because the sight of those three Santori men, standing shoulder to shoulder, tall and heart-stoppingly handsome, was so incredibly dramatic.

Of course, for every woman in the room, it was probably sheer covetous appreciation that made them stare. Because if there had ever been three finer male specimens in one place before, she'd certainly never seen them.

Ollie wasn't stupid enough to continue playing his game of let's-taunt-the-boss. He took a step back, nodding at Mike and said, "Well, guess I'll get my dinner and head to the station."

"You do that," said Mike with a tone so sharp he could probably bite through a steel plate.

The other man nodded once, turned and walked toward the front counter. Mike slowly dropped into his seat again, and his cousins did the same. The three of them remained silent, all watching the big man at the front counter, as if waiting for him to make one wrong move. Although the noise picked up around them, the tension remained at their table. Lindsey, Noelle and Izzie didn't speak, all aware their men were on edge.

After a minute or two, Ollie apparently changed his mind about dinner. He said something to the waitress and headed for the door. He did not look in their direction. She suspected he'd felt the burning heat of those stares.

When he was gone, the tension eased. It was still a long moment before Mike said, "I'm so sorry, Lindsey."

"Me, too," said Noelle. "I didn't realize you were living incognito, but I suspect I understand why."

"Why?" asked Izzie.

"I'm sure the good people of this town wouldn't be happy that the new schoolteacher is…who she is," Noelle explained in a thick whisper.

"Exactly," Lindsey said, feeling a little numb. To be honest, she didn't give a damn what anybody on Wild Boar thought of her. But she did care what they thought of Mike, and of Callie.

She had to believe, though, that people wouldn't be so unreasonable as to hold her scandalous reputation against those closest to her. Then again, people were very protective of their kids. They might read PhD, and majors in biology and chemistry after her name…but put that three-letter word, *s-e-x,* near it, too, and they flipped out.

"I need to get out of here," she said. She hadn't eaten anything, hadn't even had a chance to order, but, frankly, she'd lost her appetite.

"Let me take you home," Mike said.

"It's okay, there's no need."

"Yeah, Lindsey, there is a need," he insisted. He said to his family members, "I'm sorry, but you guys have to be on the ferry in forty minutes anyway. Can you find your way back to it?"

"Of course," Nick said. He got up, as did Mark, and they each reached out and clasped Lindsey's hand, one after the other. Their wives stood, too, offering her hugs.

Murmuring goodbye, Lindsey let Mike lead her out of the diner. She sensed they were drawing a lot of scrutiny. While she didn't recognize any faces, she had no doubt somebody from the island was eating here tonight. And even if they weren't, the staff certainly knew Mike. If they didn't recognize her yet, it wouldn't take long before they found out who she was.

Mike didn't seem to care. He kept an arm around her waist, as if daring anyone to say a word. No one did, including her and Mike, who were silent all the way home.

Once they got there, Lindsey no longer wanted to pull out their romantic picnic. She'd lost her appetite for that, too. Instead, she wondered if, in her desire to help her friend keep her job, she'd just made things worse. Her heart would break if Callie paid the price for Lindsey's storied background.

And if it hurt Mike… If he lost his job and ended up going back to Chicago, back to the police department, to a position in which he risked his life every damn day, well, she would absolutely never forgive herself. Never.

She was just tired. So very tired. Keeping all the balls up in the air, being on the roller coaster of emotions she'd been riding for months—it was all getting to her. It was early, barely seven o'clock, yet she just wanted to crawl into bed with Mike and have the kind of sex that would make days like today fade into utter insignificance.

And Mike, thankfully, was very happy to oblige her.

10

THE FIRST HINT Mike got that Ollie Dickinson had shot off his mouth came Friday afternoon. He'd been on tenterhooks all week, wondering what the jackass might have done. After several days had gone by, he'd begun to let down his guard, assuming it had blown over. Lindsey had believed the same.

Now, though, he suspected they'd been wrong.

It was around noon, the office was quiet, a lazy day with nothing moving except the dust motes floating in the air. The 911 dispatcher who ran the switchboard was on her lunch break, and one of his other officers was fielding any calls that came in.

Outside, the streets were calm, the summer people who'd come over for the holiday weekend gone for the time being. They'd return again en masse as soon as their kids got out of school, and then the streets would be crowded seven days a week. But for now, at least, Wild Boar got a respite Monday through Friday.

Which was why it was strange to see a news vehicle drive up Main Street and park in the municipal lot. He spotted it out of his window, and immediately tensed up.

Ollie had been even more cocky than usual the past

couple of days. Mike had asked him if they had a problem, and the other officer had sworn they did not, but Mike hadn't believed him.

Officer Dickinson might be as dumb as the brick wall he resembled, but even he could run an internet search. Once he had overheard that Lindsey was a doctor, and figured out she'd kept that a secret from others on the island, his curiosity must have been raised. He'd seemed a little too smug lately, and Mike had spotted him standing on the corner, talking to Mrs. Franklin the night before. The only thing that gave Mike hope Ollie hadn't discovered anything was the fact that Mrs. Franklin hadn't stormed into his office demanding information.

But now this. The Channel 8 news truck had parked, and a cameraman and reporter were climbing out of it. It wasn't the national news, far from it, just a rinky-dink station from out of Grand Rapids. Still, they'd made some effort to come across on the ferry. It was too early in the season for any locals-flock-to-the-island feel-good stories; obviously they were looking for something really juicy.

Hoping his instincts were wrong, Mike left his office and walked outside. He spotted several people peeking out from storefronts, and a couple had come outside to see what was going on.

He crossed the street, keeping a friendly expression on his face by sheer force of will as he approached the news crew. "Afternoon, folks, is there something I can do for you?"

The reporter nodded. "Yes, we're trying to find a local resident, a Dr. Lindsey Smith?"

He clenched his teeth. "Why is that?"

"We have information that she's here and we'd like to get her comment on a news story. Can you tell us how to find her?"

"Nope. That I cannot do."

Would not do. Same difference.

He suspected the youthful-looking reporter was a little savvier than her age would indicate. She realized he was hiding something and snapped her fingers at her cameraman.

"Are you Chief Santori?"

"I am. But do not turn that camera on me, ma'am. I'm not interested in any interviews."

The camera came on anyway. The reporter stuck the microphone in his face. "Chief Santori, is it true that Dr. Lindsey Smith, inventor of the Thinkgasm method, is hiding out here in your little town?"

He stared at her, not looking at the camera, or its operator, just at her. Hoping she could see exactly what he wanted to say—but wouldn't—he forced a tight smile, muttered, "No comment," then spun around and walked away.

He went into his office, picked up the phone and called the school. The secretary at the front desk greeted him cheerfully. When he apologized for calling, she reminded him that because today had been the last day of school, the students had gotten out early. They'd just left. Apparently, so had Lindsey.

Thank heaven for small favors. Her job was over, she was no longer a substitute teacher. If her real identity was discovered, at least she wouldn't have to face that ordeal. He hated to suspect the parents or administrators would turn on her, but you just never knew.

Glancing out the window, he noticed the newspeople were talking to Angie from the coffee shop, and he sent up a prayer that she was the good-natured, discreet person he'd always suspected her to be. He stepped outside. Angie caught his attention from across the street, not being obvious about it, and offered him a sly wink. The reporter, busy fiddling with her microphone, didn't notice. Nor did she look up when Angie jerked her thumb toward Mike's SUV, telling him to go.

He went.

Driving down to Lindsey's place, hoping she'd gone straight home after school, he was relieved to find her car in the driveway. He roared up the drive, pulling in behind her car.

Hopping out, he darted up the outside steps and pushed the door open without knocking. "Lindsey?"

She came out of the bedroom, wide-eyed. "Mike? What are you doing here?"

"I came to warn you. It appears Ollie did some digging and put the media on your tail. There's a news crew from Grand Rapids in town."

"Oh, God," she groaned, throwing herself down on the couch.

He went over and sat beside her, taking her into his arms. "It's going to be okay."

"It's never going to be okay," she said, sounding exhausted, mentally and physically. "This nightmare just doesn't end. When are my fifteen minutes of fame going to be over?"

"Look, you can duck the reporters. Even if they find out where you were working, school's out…there's nothing for them to attack you with."

She seemed so hopeful. "Really?"

"Definitely," he said, sure he was right.

Not thirty seconds later he heard the cars pulling up outside. And realized he'd been very, *very* wrong.

"Stay here," he told her, going to the front window and separating the curtains to gaze out. His heart sank when he recognized the Channel 8 news van. But what truly infuriated him was the vehicle leading the way—a squad car driven by Ollie Dickinson.

"That son of a bitch!"

It only got worse. Because when Ollie parked the car and got out, the passenger-side door opened, as well. Mrs. Franklin, looking both disapproving and utterly thrilled, stepped onto the driveway. "I don't believe this."

Lindsey joined him at the window. She didn't cry, didn't rant, she merely sighed heavily, as if this was exactly the moment she'd been waiting to happen all along.

She walked toward the door. "Lindsey, don't."

"I might as well face the music now. They're not going to leave until I give them something. Might as well just get it over with."

He grabbed her arm. "You don't have to do this. I'll… I'll charge them with trespassing."

"It's over, Mike. I need to do it." She lifted a hand and cupped his cheek, smiling up at him. "Thanks for trying so hard to be my knight in shining armor."

"That armor's a little tarnished right now."

"Don't you dare blame yourself. To be honest, this might be the best thing that could have happened."

"I think Ollie falling off the ferry and sinking to the bottom of the lake would have been the best thing that could have happened."

That got a tiny smile out of her, but it quickly faded. "It's time to remember who I really am and do what I do best. I've got to be strong enough to take care of myself. Just as I wrote in my dissertation, women need to take things into their own hands, so to speak."

He didn't even crack a smile at her weak joke, too worried about her to find any humor in the situation. Unable to come up with anything that would stop her, he watched her walk away, noting the stiffness of her spine, and finding her strength as amazing and remarkable as the woman herself.

He followed her, joining her at the door. The moment she pushed it open, the reporter called, "Dr. Smith! Have you really been hiding out here on Wild Boar Island for the past few months?"

"Yes, she has," Ollie said, a big, dopey grin on his face.

Mike's last strand of patience with the man just snapped. He darted down the steps, went up to his officer and grabbed him by the front of the shirt. "Get in your car and go back to town, Officer Dickinson. That's an order. Your presence here is not required."

Ollie looked at Mrs. Franklin as if he expected her to rescue him. The woman stepped up. "Officer Dickinson is the only one who seems to understand his duty to our town. He brought this ugliness to me and is the one who will handle this investigation."

Mike had had enough of the woman, too. He moved close to her. "What investigation? There is no investigation. There has been no crime!"

"Of course there has. That woman is in hiding."

Feeling as though he was talking to a wall, a really dense one, he swung around to the reporter. "Would you please inform Mrs. Franklin that you are not here chasing a criminal?"

The young woman appeared confused, gazing back and forth between them. "Well, no, of course she's not a criminal. She's famous. I'm just trying to find out why somebody who's so popular has spent the last two months twiddling her thumbs here on Wild Boar Island when she could be on any talk show in the country."

Mrs. Franklin's jaw unhinged. So did Ollie's. They both looked like they'd been doused with ice water.

Mike couldn't keep his mouth shut, and addressed all

of them. "Do any of you have any comprehension that you're tormenting a smart, decent, loving woman whose only crime was wanting to come here and help her oldest friend? You're all pathetic."

The reporter had the grace to look away. The others, well, he supposed grace was too much to ask of them.

"Now, I repeat, Officer Dickinson, get back in your car, get out of here and take her—" he gestured toward Mrs. Franklin "—with you."

She gifted him with another of her sourpuss glares. "You might be giving the orders for now, Mr. Santori, but don't expect to do so for long!"

Lindsey, who'd been watching from the porch, flew down the steps and intruded. "This has nothing to do with him. He came out here to tell me some strangers were asking about me in town, that's all. Chief Santori should be left out of this."

"Oh, sure, she's taking up for her boyfriend," said Ollie.

Sparks practically flew from her ears. She stalked toward the man, enraged and brilliant, and got right in his face. "I'm going to be going into town today and filing a sexual-harassment suit against you."

Mrs. Franklin looked stunned. Ollie just looked ready to piss his pants.

"This man is a menace," she snapped, staring down Mrs. Franklin. "He's harassed me and other women in this community."

"Now, listen here, lady, you just mistook friendliness for something it wasn't," Ollie said, the explanation sounding pathetic and weak.

Lindsey wasn't finished. "Two of the other teachers at the school have told me he's pulled them over for no other reason than to hit on them. I, for one, am not going to allow him to continue such behavior, and I'll be filing a complaint."

The president of the town council seemed properly scandalized, the reporter interested.

Ollie tried to explain, but Mrs. Franklin, perhaps noticing the cameraman lift his camera, cut off his explanations. "That will be all, Ollie. You can take me back into town, and together, we'll be stopping by to visit your uncle. I suspect he'll have something to say about this behavior."

Huh. Mike suddenly remembered something. Mrs. Franklin, long a widow, was supposedly very friendly with Ollie's uncle, the former chief. He had to wonder if the woman had been doing some meddling, trying to get her boyfriend's nephew the job he'd wanted but had been denied.

But she wasn't entirely distracted by Ollie's bad behavior. Casting a sour look at Mike, she said, "I expect the council will be calling you to come in to make a full report."

"I'll give it its due attention," he said with a deliberate eye roll, watching as the utterly unlikable duo got into the car and drove away. Frankly, he didn't give a damn about her, the council, Ollie, or his job. He just wanted Lindsey to be okay.

He turned to tell her that, to let her know he'd be right there by her side throughout this ordeal, but saw to his surprise that she was no longer standing beside him on the lawn. Instead, she was on the porch, opening the door and ushering in the reporter and her cameraman. She had a smile on her face—a weak, rather forced one—but it was full of determination.

Lindsey had finally reached some point of no return. She was taking control of the situation that had been controlling her for months.

He went up the steps. She stood in the doorway.

"Are you all right?"

"I'll be fine, Mike. This is long overdue."

"Do you need me to stay?"

"No. Thank you, for everything, but I've got to do this last part on my own."

He saw that steel in her, the unmistakable strength, and knew she was right. She had to face the challenge and be the one to beat it. Although it was hard to not keep fighting for her, to not be her protector, he had to let her go. So, with a nod and a brush of his lips on her temple, he spun around, walked down the steps and drove away.

LINDSEY MANAGED TO retain her calm throughout the entire hour-long interview. She didn't cry, she didn't bitch, she didn't criticize anyone—not other reporters, not her bosses. She was entirely professional, holding on to her emotions with ruthless determination. She had the bloody palms—from clenching her fists so hard—to prove it.

The young reporter was actually very nice and respectful. Once she realized Lindsey was going to give her a scoop—the real story of why the infamous sex doctor had dropped out of sight—she'd been very easy to get along with. She hadn't exactly asked softball questions, but she'd respected Lindsey's privacy where possible—including not asking about Mike.

All in all, Lindsey was happy with how it had gone. The local audience might be the only one who ever watched it, but she seriously doubted it. This thing might not get picked up on the national networks, but it would hit the internet—of that she was sure.

Perhaps it would do some good. Maybe when people saw her as a calm, rational, thoughtful professional, they'd stop focusing on orgasms and start focusing on the real issue the PhD had been talking about. That was her hope, anyway.

Of course, her bosses were going to be furious. Far from obeying the edict to stay out of the limelight, she'd sought it out and leaped into it, feet first.

But she realized she didn't care. She was tired of being reactive instead of proactive, tired of letting others dictate where she went, what she did and how she was supposed to behave. She'd behaved so differently from the Lindsey she'd always been, she almost didn't recognize herself.

Well, that was over. Done. Even if it cost her her job. Screw it, there were other jobs. She was through being pushed around.

After the reporter and her cameraman had departed, Lindsey was left with some decisions to make. Her first instinct was to call Mike and ask him to come back. There was no one else in the world she wanted to share this moment of quiet triumph with more than him. She might not have won the war, but, damn it, she'd at least picked up a weapon and fought for herself.

But whenever she reached for the phone, two things kept flashing into her mind.

First, she'd just congratulated herself on reclaiming the real her. She was in control again, a one-woman island, strong and determined. How could she regress to leaning on someone else…especially someone else who just wanted to have an affair with her?

If Mike loved her—if he'd told her he loved her, as she now knew she loved him—it might be different. People in love, who were in committed, long-term relationships, *should* rely on each other. She and Mike didn't have that, though, no matter how much she might want it. It was high time she remembered that, and stuck to relying only on herself, just as she'd always done.

Second, she kept seeing Mrs. Franklin's face and hearing her voice. She'd said the town council would want to speak to him. In other words, the town council would be firing him.

That was her fault. If she'd never come here, Mike's job would never have been at risk. He'd have finished his probationary period, secured a permanent position and melted right into island life. He'd probably have met a nice woman and had that pot-roast-and-picket-fence lifestyle he'd once mentioned.

Now it was all ruined, because of her.

He would lose his job. Considering his family and friends were all in Chicago, that would be the first place he'd consider retreating to. If she were still a part of his life, her presence there would only add to that instinctive reaction.

Once he was in Chicago, how long would it be before he had to get into the line of work she knew he loved? He might not want to get shot at, but being a cop was part of who he was. He'd end up back on the Chicago P.D. Back in the line of fire.

"No," she whispered, heartsick at the very thought of it. Even if she was just his short-term, sexy fling, no way did she want him to ever put himself into more dangerous situations.

She couldn't let it happen. She just couldn't.

Finally, knowing she had to do something about it, she got on the phone and made several phone calls. She skipped Mrs. Franklin, well aware that was a lost cause. But she had met the other members of the town council over the past couple of months, and believed them to be nice and reasonable men.

She told them all her story, stressing how little Mike had to do with her presence here on the island. She made sure they understood that he'd had no idea who she was or what she did for a living when she'd accepted the job at the school. She said she'd tried to offer her full credentials to the school administrators, who hadn't seemed the least bit interested. And she finished by reminding them it would be patently unfair for Mike to get any of the blame for whatever notoriety she brought on the town, and that under no circumstances should Callie be blamed, either, since she'd been in the middle of a horribly stressful personal situation.

They'd been very nice. Very understanding.

And, when they found out what her big secret was, very flirtatious. Dirty old dogs.

By the time she'd hung up from the last call, she was confident that Mrs. Franklin wasn't going to get her way as far as Mike Santori went. The fact that she'd told every one of the council members about Ollie's nightmarish tactics with women would help, too. Ollie's uncle, the former chief, might support him, but nobody on the town council did, other than Mrs. Franklin. And after today, even her support might be tenuous.

Finally, when Lindsey was sure she'd done all she could, she began to pack. She threw her things in boxes and dumped them in her car. The phone rang twice. She checked the caller ID and ignored Callie's call, and then Mike's. Hearing a loving, consoling voice might make her feel better, but it wouldn't help her do what had to be done.

She had to leave. Now.

She would go back to the mainland. She'd already turned in her final grades for her students... There was nothing holding her here. It was time—past time—to go home and try to reclaim her life. If her bosses didn't want her, well, there were other clinics. Maybe more progressive ones where women's sexual issues weren't treated as a joke.

She could go back to the real her—self-reliant, self-controlled, not needing anyone. Well, at least, not *allowing* herself to need anyone.

Meanwhile, Mike's life could return to normal. He could stay here, happily. *Safely.* Without her.

Her heart was breaking as she finished loading up the car. It cracked completely when she sat down to write him a note, explaining why she'd left. He might never forgive her for leaving like this, without having the guts to say goodbye to his face. The trouble was, if she saw him, she wouldn't be *able* to say goodbye. She simply loved him too much.

She propped the note on the doorknob, knowing he'd come to the cottage tonight when he didn't hear from her. Then she got in the car.

Sitting behind the wheel, the enormity of everything that had happened this afternoon washed over her. She felt drained, physically and emotionally. She suspected she might be experiencing a hint of shock, but forced herself to keep moving forward.

But not until she'd cried a little.

Or a lot.

Once the long-held-in tears began to flow freely from her eyes, she found them impossible to stop.

It had been a long time since she'd really cried. Such a long time. These weren't quiet, soft tears, either. This was ugly, raw, violent sobbing. Her throat hurt, her eyes hurt and a glance in the rearview mirror revealed she looked as hideous as she felt.

"Get it together, girl," she told herself as she glanced at the clock. She wanted to catch the 7:00 p.m. ferry. If she waited, Mike would stop her from catching the later one.

She rubbed her eyes with her sleeve, switched the car

on and drove away from the little cottage where she and Mike had spent so many blissful, passionate hours.

The thought that she would never be with him again almost made her skip the turn for the landing and keep going up to town, just so she could see him one more time.

She knew better, though. So she turned.

The landing was actually pretty crowded, as lots of people were coming over from the mainland for the weekend. Few, however, were taking the return trip. In fact, hers was the only car loaded on by the crew.

The captain, who she'd met on her previous trips, offered her a big smile and said, "Come on aboard, miss! Gonna have the whole lounge to yourself tonight."

The lounge consisted of a dingy cabin with a few bench seats and a couple of vending machines. She'd rather take her chances on deck, even if there was no handsome, charming man to convince her not to jump overboard if she got too seasick this time.

Walking up on deck, she watched as the crew finished readying to sail. Dusk was approaching, the late spring day coming to a close. But it was still light enough to easily see the shoreline, and she could visualize the cute little town beyond it.

There wasn't much wind tonight, and just a light chop. She hoped that meant she wouldn't be sick over the side, but wasn't ruling anything out.

"Off we go!" cried the captain to his crew, and she gripped the railing, saying her goodbyes as the engines roared to life.

But before they slipped out of the dock, she spied a vehicle approaching the landing. It sped across the parking lot, spewing gravel, flashing its lights.

Not just its headlights, but its police light, as well.

A few loud blurps accompanied it.

"Oh, God," she whispered, knowing it was Mike.

He'd gotten her note too soon and was coming to… what? To ask her to stay? How could she stay when she was so out of place here, when her career was such a holy scandal?

Besides, she didn't want to live on Wild Boar Island. She had no chance of a career here. And while the people were nice enough, and she'd love to visit again, she hated living like a butterfly in a box.

Mike was building a new life here; he had a job that was safe and steady, where he could really work toward a future. There was no room for her in that life, or that future. God, why couldn't he have just let her go?

"Seems there might be a problem," the captain said, calling down from the upper deck. "We'll have to delay for a few minutes."

"Oh, please don't," she said, wondering if he could see the tears tracking down her cheeks. She just didn't have the strength to say goodbye to Mike's face.

"Sorry, miss. That's Chief Santori. Gotta find out what he wants."

It was hopeless, so she stayed still, watching as Mike pulled up to the very edge of the dock. The ferry gate was up, blocking his passage, but Mike rolled the window down and yelled up to the captain. "Sorry to be late, but I really need to get on board."

"Is it an emergency?"

He looked away from the captain, staring at her through the windshield. Finally, he yelled back, "It is to me."

"That'll do, then," the captain said. He glanced back toward her, and Lindsey figured he'd noticed the comings and goings of her and the chief. They might have fooled some people by pretending to travel apart, but the captain had to have noticed that whenever one of them went across on the ferry, the other one did, too.

Lindsey wrapped her arms around herself, trying to maintain her calm as the captain lowered the gate and sent one of the crew members over to drive the SUV on board. As soon as he relinquished the wheel, Mike strode up the gangplank, heading straight for her. He was so handsome, his hair windblown, his strong body looking amazing in soft, loose-fitting jeans and a dark T-shirt. The man was even more delicious out of uniform. Of course, he was most delicious out of clothes altogether.

Stop it. Don't think about him that way.

His steps slowed as he drew closer.

"Mike, *what* are you doing here?"

"Oh, Lindsey, wow, fancy running into you here. Did you remember to take your Dramamine?"

"Why did you follow me?"

"What makes you think I followed you?" he asked with a shrug so nonchalant she almost wanted to smack him. How he could be so calm and casual when she was a churning mass of ugly emotion?

"I'll ask you again. What are you doing here?"

"Why do you care?" he asked, his voice finally revealing something other than that forced good humor. She heard anger there, and perhaps hurt.

Damn it. Of course she'd hurt him. She'd been a coward and left him only a note, after everything they'd shared over the past couple of months. The fact that she'd done it because she was scared to need someone so much, and even more scared for his very life probably wouldn't have occurred to him.

"I care," she said softly. "I care more than I ever wanted to."

That seemed to anger him more. He grabbed her upper

arms, none too gently, and pulled her close. "You have a hell of a way of showing it."

She closed her eyes, sucking her bottom lip into her mouth, trying to find the words that would make him let her go without making him decide to do something she didn't even want him to think about doing. Namely, coming back to Chicago to be with her, and returning to his old lifestyle.

In the end, though, there was only the truth. Lindsey had never been a liar; she just wasn't good at it.

"Mike, I meant what I said in the note. I'm leaving because I have to get on my own feet again and start taking control of my own destiny."

"Who's stopping you?"

"Not you," she insisted, not wanting him to think she blamed him. "It's just become so easy to let my feelings for you dictate what I'm doing."

He said nothing.

"I was also being honest about not wanting to be the one to cost you the life you're building for yourself. I've caused you nothing but trouble, and if you lose your job and have to stop doing something you really want to do because of me, I just couldn't live with it."

His grip loosened a little. He continued to stare searchingly into her face, his eyes lit by the setting sun that turned them to amber.

"There's more. Tell me the rest."

"What?"

"Let down the walls. Stop holding back. Say what you *really* feel and tell me what you *really* want." He lifted a hand and stroked her cheek. "Please, Lindsey. Don't keep protecting yourself, not from me. You don't have to be afraid to show me the real you."

Knowing what he was asking of her, Lindsey trembled.

Was she being a coward? Was this all based on fear? Her fear of losing him, of him being hurt, even her fear of actually having to come out and admit she loved him?

Was running away, making excuses that it was for his own good, all *really* about her inability to actually trust him with her heart?

"I love you," she whispered, the words barely rising from her lips.

He stepped closer. "What?"

She swallowed, gathering her strength. "I love you, Mike. I love you so much, but loving you has made me almost forget who I am. I'm too vulnerable to you."

He cupped her face in his hands, staring at her, his eyes filled with tenderness. "Do you trust me, Lindsey? Do you trust me with every bit of yourself—your secrets, your dreams, your dark thoughts, your fondest memories?"

She considered, but not for long. Nodding, she revealed what was in her heart. "Yes, I do." She breathed deeply, feeling as though a weight had been lifted. "I really do. I love you so much, and I can't imagine my life without you, which, frankly, scares me to death. And I hate being scared, damn it! I just hate—"

He cut her off, covering her mouth with his, kissing her deeply, tenderly, as if he wanted to take away her fear and her doubts and savor only the admission that she loved him. She clung to him, their bodies melting together on the edge of the ferry, close to where they'd first met. The craft might have started moving, or they might still be at the dock. She didn't know, and she didn't care. She'd given him the truth, and she'd admitted it to herself.

He was a man she could trust with every ounce of herself, heart, mind and body.

He ended the kiss to whisper, "I love you. I'm crazy, wildly, madly in love with you."

She couldn't help smiling, even as tears pricked her eyes again. So strange to be such a weepy woman after all these years of stoicism. So strange to be smiling after so much confusion.

How could she not smile, though? Mike loved her. Really loved her. This hadn't been just a fling for him, any more than it had been for her. She felt as though someone had given her a precious gift, one she'd protect and cherish for as long as she lived.

He lifted his hand and brushed a tear off her cheek with the tip of his finger. "I love the strong, independent, powerful you. I would never want you to change. And if I've done anything to make you think I don't love that wonderful part of you, please feel free to slap me."

"Never."

"I think you're utterly magnificent, Lindsey Smith, and I can't imagine spending my life with any other woman in the world."

"Really?" she whispered, reminding herself of something she'd always told her patients—it's great to be self-reliant. But when you find someone who you can really entrust with your body, your soul, your hopes and your dreams, you will only become stronger because of that union.

"I'll stay here," she told him. She couldn't possibly leave him, not now that she knew he loved her as much as she loved him. "I'll find a way to work from here, write a book, or travel and do lectures and then come home to you."

He hugged her tightly, stroking her back, twining his other hand in her long hair, which was blowing on the evening breeze. "I love the idea of you always coming home to me, but that won't be necessary."

"What do you mean?" Suddenly fearful, she pulled

away and looked up at him. "They didn't fire you, did they?"

He shook his head. Before she could breathe a sigh of relief, though, he added, "They didn't have to. I quit."

She flinched so hard, she almost stumbled. He grabbed her, preventing her from falling.

"You're joking."

"Nope. I'm entirely serious. I promised I'd stay for the last several weeks of my probationary period, but after that, I'm gone."

"Oh, God, no, Mike. Please tell me you didn't do this for me. I wouldn't be able to stand it if you went back to the police force in Chicago." She gripped the front of his shirt, shaking him. "You will not put your life in danger for me!"

He shook his head, taking her hands and squeezing them between his. Hers were a little cold, and he rubbed them gently.

"I'm not going back to the Chicago P.D."

"What will you do?" she asked, wondering if both of them were about to be standing in the unemployment line.

"My cousins want me to go into business with them," Mike said.

She gasped, relief filling her from head to toe. "Are you serious?"

"Very serious."

Not even trying to keep the relief out of her voice, she asked, "What kind of business?"

"Private security," he explained. "Mark's leaving the force—Noelle's had as much as she can stand of it, too. He's a dad now...he can't be doing that stuff."

She didn't blame the woman at all. It must be hard to raise children with a man who was at that much risk every day on the job.

"As for Nick, he's tired of doing the club thing. But it

did give him a lot of private-security experience, plus he has a military background."

"It sounds like they've got a plan."

"A good one. They've already got clients lined up. It won't be the same as being the chief of police in Tinytown, USA, but I won't be on the streets of Chicago, either. I guess it's what you'd call a happy medium."

That sounded fine to her. In fact, it sounded perfect.

She wanted him to be happy, wanted him to do what he enjoyed doing. Wanting him safe, however, outweighed everything else.

"I think the three of us are going to make one hell of a team."

"They can be your away team," she told him, wrapping her arms around his waist. "How about we leave the home team at just two players."

He kissed her tenderly, whispering, "I love you so much."

"And I love you, sweet man."

She wrapped her arms around his waist and held tight as their kiss went on and on. Lindsey was so relieved, and so blissfully happy, she felt like she could fly.

Realizing they were at sail, heading toward the other coast, it seemed as though they really *were* flying. The wind whipped them, the water lapped at the ferry, but this time, there was no dizziness, no unsteadiness.

She was in Mike's arms, right where she was meant to be.

Epilogue

Seven Months Later

WAKING UP ON Christmas Eve morning, Lindsey reached across the bed, feeling for Mike, but found his side empty. She frowned, then sniffed, smelling something delicious, and remembered he'd promised to make her breakfast in bed.

He knew this would be her first real Christmas, and he wanted to make it as perfect as he possibly could. His thoughtfulness, his tenderness, was on display every day.

As for the nights. Oh, wow, the nights.

She would never tire of making love with that man. Some nights were lazy and lethargic, others wild and erotic. She found herself enjoying the submissive role quite a lot. What woman wouldn't want to be forced to stay still and take whatever amazing pleasures her lover wanted to give to her?

It was something she sometimes discussed with her clients. Now that she was back at work full-time, happily employed by a clinic here in Chicago that considered her an asset rather than a liability, she found she enjoyed her job much more. Mike's new business was thriving, the only drawback being they both worked long hours.

But when they were home, in their cute downtown apartment, they made up for the hours apart in every way possible.

Smiling, she curled up under the covers, just thinking about all the delicious things they'd done together in this bed the night before.

She thought, and thought, and thought, and…nothing happened. "Oh, well," she sighed. Apparently she still needed her man to satisfy her.

Frankly, though, despite the popularity of the Think-gasm method, which had really gained traction when the interview she'd done had been picked up by the main-stream, she wouldn't have it any other way. Nothing could ever compare to being entirely intimate and open—with no walls or barriers—with the man she loved.

But thinking about him was still *very* nice.

So nice that she had a Cheshire-cat smile on her face when Mike walked into the room a few minutes later, car-rying a tray.

"Happy Christmas Eve!"

She sat up in the bed, smiling at him as he put the tray on her lap. He'd apparently gone all out, because the plate was covered by a giant metal dome, like something out of a restaurant.

"You're so good to me."

"I hope you like it."

"I'm sure it'll taste delicious."

He grimaced. "Well, I'm not sure about that."

"You're a wonderful cook."

"Yeah, but I just don't know if this particular thing is what you want for breakfast. It's not your average bacon and eggs."

Her interest piqued, she reached for the handle on the top of the dome. Mike watched her closely, his eyes dancing with secret amusement, which just increased her curiosity.

She removed the cover, and had to blink a few times to make sure she was seeing what she thought she was seeing.

"Is that a…"

"Yes, it is," he said, joining her on the bed and reaching for the object that sat alone on the white plate.

It was a ring. A perfect, beautiful ring. Platinum with a large, square-cut emerald, simple and stark, it needed no other stones or adornments to be the most beautiful thing she'd ever laid eyes upon.

He lifted it, and stared into her face, letting her see the oceans of love he felt for her.

"Will you marry me, Lindsey?"

She nodded. "Yes. Oh, yes, I will."

He slid the ring onto her left hand then kissed her almost reverently. In midkiss, Lindsey sniffed, her eyes welling up. Damned if Mike hadn't turned her into an emotional watering can. He could make her cry with delight, with pleasure and with utter, overwhelming tenderness.

Some analyst might conclude she'd met the man of her dreams and was wildly in love for the first—and last—time of her life.

And they'd be right.

* * * * *

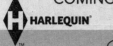

REQUEST YOUR FREE BOOKS!
2 FREE NOVELS PLUS 2 FREE GIFTS!

HARLEQUIN®

Blaze®

red-hot reads!

YES! Please send me 2 FREE Harlequin® Blaze™ novels and my 2 FREE gifts (gifts are worth about $10). After receiving them, if I don't wish to receive any more books, I can return the shipping statement marked "cancel." If I don't cancel, I will receive 4 brand-new novels every month and be billed just $4.74 per book in the U.S. or $4.96 per book in Canada. That's a savings of at least 14% off the cover price. It's quite a bargain. Shipping and handling is just 50¢ per book in the U.S. and 75¢ per book in Canada.* I understand that accepting the 2 free books and gifts places me under no obligation to buy anything. I can always return a shipment and cancel at any time. Even if I never buy another book, the two free books and gifts are mine to keep forever.

150/350 HDN F4WC

Name _____ (PLEASE PRINT) _____

Address _____ Apt. # _____

City _____ State/Prov. _____ Zip/Postal Code _____

Signature (if under 18, a parent or guardian must sign) _____

Mail to the **Harlequin® Reader Service:**
IN U.S.A.: P.O. Box 1867, Buffalo, NY 14240-1867
IN CANADA: P.O. Box 609, Fort Erie, Ontario L2A 5X3

Want to try two free books from another line?
Call 1-800-873-8635 or visit www.ReaderService.com.

* Terms and prices subject to change without notice. Prices do not include applicable taxes. Sales tax applicable in N.Y. Canadian residents will be charged applicable taxes. Offer not valid in Quebec. This offer is limited to one order per household. Not valid for current subscribers to Harlequin Blaze books. All orders subject to credit approval. Credit or debit balances in a customer's account(s) may be offset by any other outstanding balance owed by or to the customer. Please allow 4 to 6 weeks for delivery. Offer available while quantities last.

Your Privacy—The Harlequin® Reader Service is committed to protecting your privacy. Our Privacy Policy is available online at www.ReaderService.com or upon request from the Harlequin Reader Service.

We make a portion of our mailing list available to reputable third parties that offer products we believe may interest you. If you prefer that we not exchange your name with third parties, or if you wish to clarify or modify your communication preferences, please visit us at www.ReaderService.com/consumerchoice or write to us at Harlequin Reader Service Preference Service, P.O. Box 9062, Buffalo, NY 14269. Include your complete name and address.

Riding High

"Caution. Proceeding with it."

"You want to proceed?"

"I do." Her eyes darkened to midnight-blue and her gentle sigh was filled to the brim with surrender as her arms slid around his neck, depositing mud along the way.

As if he gave a damn. His body hummed with anticipation. "Me, too." Slowly he lowered his head and closed his eyes.

"Mistake, though."

He hovered near her mouth, hardly daring to breathe. Had she changed her mind at the last minute? "Why?"

"Tell you later." She brought his head down and made the connection.

And it was as electric as he'd imagined. His blood fizzed as it raced through his body and eventually settled in his groin. Her lips fit perfectly against his from the first moment of contact. It seemed his mouth had been created for kissing Lily, and vice versa.

He tried a different angle, just to test that theory. Still perfect, still high-voltage. Since they were standing in water, it was a wonder they didn't short out. He couldn't speak for her but he'd bet he was glowing. His skin was hot enough to send off sparks.

She moaned and pressed her body closer. She felt amazing in his arms—soft, wet and slippery. He'd never imagined doing it in the mud, but suddenly that seemed like the best idea in the world.

Then she snorted. Odd. Not the reaction he would have expected considering where this seemed to be heading.

He lifted his head and gazed into her flushed face. "Did you just laugh?"

She regarded him with passion-filled eyes. "That wasn't me."

"Then who—"

The snort came again as something bumped the back of his knees. A heavy splash sent water up the back of his legs.

She might not have been laughing before but she was now. "Um, we have company."

Although it didn't matter which pig had interrupted the moment, Regan had his money on Harley. Whichever one had decided to take an after-dinner mud bath, they'd ruined what had been a very promising kiss.

Pick up RIDING HIGH by Vicki Lewis Thompson, available June 2014 wherever Harlequin® Blaze® books are sold!

And don't miss RIDING HARD and RIDING HOME in July and August of 2014!

HBEXP79803

It feels good to be bad!

Good girl and preacher's daughter Melanie Knowles has lived a sheltered life in Blackfoot Falls, Montana. No one could ever imagine she has a secret thing for bad boys... that is until ex-con Lucas Sloan comes to town.

Don't miss the latest in the
Made in Montana miniseries

Need You Now

by reader-favorite author
Debbi Rawlins

Available June 2014 wherever you buy
Harlequin Blaze books.

Fires aren't all that's sizzling for this smoking-hot firefighter!

Firefighter Dylan Cross, aka Mr. June in the annual "hottie" calendar, is used to risking his life to save others. But he's not about to risk his heart—or his bachelorhood!—when it comes to sexy Cassie Price....

From the reader-favorite miniseries *Last Bachelor Standing*

The Final Score
by Nancy Warren

Available June 2014 wherever you buy
Harlequin Blaze books.

Available now from the
Last Bachelor Standing miniseries by Nancy Warren

Game On
Breakaway